THE FAMILY FLETCHER TAKES ROCK ISLAND

ALSO BY DANA ALISON LEVY

The Misadventures of the Family Fletcher

THE FAMILY FLETCHER TAKES ROCK ISLAND

DANA ALISON LEVY

DELACORTE PRESS

This is a work of fiction. Names, characters, places, and incidents either are the product of the author's imagination or are used fictitiously. Any resemblance to actual persons, living or dead, events, or locales is entirely coincidental.

 Published in the United States by Delacorte Press, an imprint of Random House Children's Books, a division of Penguin Random House LLC, New York.

Delacorte Press is a registered trademark and the colophon is a trademark of Penguin Random House LLC.

randomhousekids.com

Educators and librarians, for a variety of teaching tools, visit us at RHTeachersLibrarians.com

Library of Congress Cataloging-in-Publication Data
Names: Levy, Dana Alison, author.
Title: The family Fletcher takes Rock Island / Dana Alison Levy.
Description: First edition. | New York: Delacorte Press, [2016] | Summary: Summertime brings the Fletcher Family back to Rock Island where the good times never end, but this summer the boys' favorite lighthouse is all boarded up and with the help from their new neighbors, the Garcia girls, the boys are determined to find out what is really happening with their lighthouse and saving it, no matter what the cost.
Identifiers: LCCN 2015014134 | ISBN 978-0-553-52130-6 (hc) | ISBN 978-0-553-52131-3 (glb) | ISBN 978-0-553-52132-0 (ebook)
Subjects: | CYAC: Family—Alternative Family—Fiction. | Social Issues—Fiction. | Humorous Stories—Fiction.

The text of this book is set in 12.2-point Sabon MT.
Interior design by Stephanie Moss

Printed in the United States of America
10 9 8 7 6 5 4 3 2 1
First Edition

Random House Children's Books supports the First Amendment and celebrates the right to read.

For Eri, with love and gratitude for all those glorious summers.
You are the best big sister in the whole wide world.

Chapter One

IN WHICH WE ARRIVE BACK AT ROCK ISLAND, A PLACE WHERE TIME STANDS STILL

CAPTAIN JIM'S ISLAND NEWS
August 1, 6:00 a.m.

Should be another beautiful day on Rock Island, with temperatures in the low eighties and a strong breeze for the sailors. And speaking of sailors, anybody own a black Labrador retriever named Gus? If so, please come to the Coast Guard station. Gus got tangled in some rigging and has been slobbering all over the Coast Guard yeoman since his heroic rescue.

"We're going to miss the boat!" Frog wailed from the back of the van. He was buckled in the third row with Sir Puggleton the dog and two cat carriers housing Zeus, the eighteen-pound Maine coon, and Lili, the six-month-old marmalade kitten. All were yowling the low, discontented yowls of animals resigned to their plight. Frog's three older brothers were crammed in the middle seats, also occasionally yowling. No one was happy.

"We have time. We'll make it," Dad said. But Eli noticed him twist his head to peer at the traffic clogging the highway.

"Of course we'll make it!" Papa boomed. He was leaning forward as he drove, as though he could plow through the traffic by sheer force of will. "We've never missed a ferry yet."

"Yes we have!"

Jax and Eli spoke at the same time.

Eli shot a glance at his older brother and let him do the talking. Jax could be counted on to get the facts right.

"Remember, Papa? When we were supposed to go for Memorial Day one year? And there was an accident on the highway? And we sat—"

"We sat for FOUR HOURS," Sam interjected, pausing his mad texting and looking up briefly from his phone. "And I missed a soccer tournament that weekend. That was the worst."

"Yeah, and Sir Puggleton barfed in the car," Frog added.

"And we had to stay in that gross motel," Eli said, his nose wrinkling at the memory.

"Ah yes, the Mildew Inn, I think we named it. Happy family memories, eh, guys?" Dad asked.

"Gentlemen, please. We are only around ten minutes

from the dock. We have plenty of time. Maybe not as much time as we would have had if *someone* hadn't neglected to put his suitcase in the car, requiring us to turn around and pick it up"—here Papa paused and stared pointedly at Dad—"but we still have time. Fear not."

Sure enough, just as he finished speaking, Papa moved the car into the exit lane and down the ramp. Eli knew they were close. Jax and Sam both lowered their windows and the thick, warm, salty ocean air rushed through the chill of the air-conditioned car. Sir Puggleton started barking in earnest, knowing freedom was near.

Eli closed his eyes and let the smell overwhelm him as the car made the last few turns to the ferry dock. It was the smell of a working harbor, of diesel engines and fish and seagulls and fried seafood from the restaurant next to the ferry. It was the smell of August, when the Fletcher family boarded the ferry and crossed the twenty miles of Atlantic Ocean that separated the mainland from Rock Island. They were almost there.

Of course, first they had to actually get on the boat.

"Frog. FROG! Please, hold someone's hand! Don't run ahead!" Dad called. His arms were full of tote bags and coolers, and he moved at a slow shuffle that couldn't match Frog's excited leaps. Papa was still in the long, snaking line, waiting to drive the car into the belly of the boat.

"Jax, get your brother please," Dad ordered as Frog dodged around a startled-looking elderly couple and ran toward the gangplank.

"Can't Sam get him? I've got this stupid furry moron," Jax said, hefting Lili's cat carrier, where she was caterwauling as though being tortured.

"Well, I've got THIS furry moron," Sam retorted. His arm was straining from the weight of Zeus's carrier. "But fine. Just take my ball, then," he said, booting the soccer ball toward Jax and running to catch up with Frog. Jax bellowed and lurched forward to try to catch the ball before it rolled off the edge of the dock and into the water. Clearly disliking the jerky movements, Lili wailed louder.

"This stupid kitten!" Jax said. He tucked the ball securely under one arm and tried to steady the swinging cat carrier. "Why won't she just zip it?"

"You upset her," Eli said. "Animals communicate very clearly without words, you know. She's using the language she has to tell you she's scared." He was pulling Sir Puggleton, whose nails were scraping the gangplank in an effort to stay on solid land. Sir Puggleton loathed boats, and his preferred language seemed to be an utter refusal to move.

Jax shrugged. "She's upsetting me with these noises,

but—" Suddenly Lili made a desperate gacking sound. "EW! What kind of 'secret message' does cat gack send?"

"Let's just get on the boat, boys. We can clean everything up then." Dad looked rattled, and Eli noticed there was nobody anywhere near them on the dock.

"Frogface! Get over here now!" Sam ordered, and reluctantly, Frog turned. Sam was pretty much the only Fletcher brother who could get Frog to listen.

"But I can see minnows! And crabs way down low," he said.

"We can see them on the island. You don't want to miss the ferry, do you? We can leave you behind if you want. . . ."

Frog shrieked and ran to grab Sam's hand. More or less pulled together, the Fletchers stood in line to get on the boat.

Eli glanced around. They were taking up the whole gangplank. First was Sam, who at thirteen was practically as tall as a grown-up. He was shaggy, with his summer-vacation-means-no-haircuts rule, and he looked even bigger standing next to Frog, who, even though he was six and a half, was still smaller than the other soon-to-be first-graders at his school. In the summer, Sam's skin tanned enough that he didn't look as pale next to Frog, but they still didn't look like brothers. Of course, thought Eli, neither did he and Jax. Jax had shaved off his Afro at the end of the school year, deciding it was too hot for summer. But Eli's pale skin freckled and burned, while Jax started out dark and just got darker. And Jax didn't have glasses sliding down his sweaty nose far more than he would like. At least Eli was still taller than Jax, although Jax liked to point out that he would always be five months older.

They walked up the gangplank and the narrow metal stairs of the boat, their voices echoing and their feet clanging. Finally, *finally,* the Fletchers emerged way up high on the top deck, the sunlight making them squint after the darkness of the stairwell. Squeezing and shoving, they shuffled onto a group of deck chairs and dropped their bundles with a sigh.

The boat picked up speed once it exited the harbor. As always, Frog covered his ears and buried his face in Papa's lap when the loud horn sounded. Then they were finally on their way. Slowly, the mainland got smaller and smaller behind them, disappearing into the fog that was somehow dim and bright at the same time. Salty dampness coated their skin.

Papa sighed a deep, happy sigh. "Nothing in this world is as good as the moment when the Rock Island ferry leaves the dock. For over forty years I've been taking this ferry, and Mimi and Boppa probably took it a dozen times before that. Nothing but sand, rocks, sea, and sky at the other end."

"And ice cream," Frog added. "And all the crabs and

lobsters! Do you think Gar Baby will be there?" Gar Baby was his cherished hermit crab from last summer.

"Crabs don't tend to live long," Eli started to say. "Seagulls and other predators—"

"Yes indeed! Well, let's not dwell on the carnivorous habits of seagulls right now, okay, E-man?" Papa interrupted. He cast a worried look at Frog, who had been known to sob uncontrollably when faced with nature's harder lessons. "How about that ice cream! What flavor will you get?"

"Coffee fudge, like always," Eli said decisively.

The rest of the boys answered quickly.

"Chocolate."

"Cookie dough."

"Soft-serve swirl."

"I kind of wish they'd get some new flavors," Sam said. "They've had the same stuff forever." He sighed. "And there's literally no phone service anywhere."

Papa gave him a look, and Sam quickly continued. "But still. I can't wait to get there! I wonder how the surf's been. I bet I'll catch some sick rides this year."

"And who wants new flavors anyway?" Jax asked, sounding defensive of the island. "It's perfect the way it is. The best ice cream, the best tide pools, the best lighthouse . . . Why would you want it to change?"

"Hey, I call the lighthouse first!" Sam yelled, forgetting his phone for a minute. "You guys can go downstairs, but I get first climb."

"No way! We can all go up. I want to see if there are any seals off the rocks and that's the only place to see them," Eli said.

"Yeah, and I want to have a water battle, upstairs versus downstairs," Jax said. "Downstairs gets the hose!"

The lighthouse, with its massive striped exterior, was maybe the very best part of Rock Island. It sat right next door to the Fletchers' house, and its empty interior, complete with winding staircase, was open to the public. And on their end of the island, the public meant the Fletchers. The only other houses nearby were a giant sea captain's mansion that had sat empty for years, owned by some people who lived far away, and tiny cottages filled with old couples who had no interest in a lighthouse. The Fletcher house was tiny too—a fishing shack that had been built up over the years to its current size of two bedrooms and a sleeping loft. But who cared how tiny it was when they could escape to the lighthouse next door?

"We'll go up all together, same as always," Jax said. Sam nodded, overruled.

Eli sighed with satisfaction. He loved Rock Island, the sameness of each summer, the activities that had turned into traditions and now felt like important rituals: the first run up the lighthouse stairs, the first ice cream cone, the first dunk in the waves. "Same as always," he said, echoing Jax.

"I want everything to stay exactly the same forever and

ever," Frog said. He was cuddled against Papa, half-asleep from the rocking of the boat.

"Things have to change a little," Dad said, speaking up from where he lay across a bench, a sweatshirt making a pillow under his head. "Look at you guys. Another year older, and bigger, and looking for new adventures."

Jax shook his head. "No! Rock Island doesn't change. Their sign even says it: 'Welcome to Rock Island, Where Time Stands Still.' It's always the same. And that's why I love it."

Chapter Two

IN WHICH THE GOOD, THE BAD, AND THE ICE CREAM ALL SHOW UP

August 1

To: LucyCupcake

From: PapaBear

Subject: MADE IT

Hey, Luce—

We are officially on the ferry, which, between attempting to pack at midnight last night and the traffic this morning, feels like a victory. Who knows what we forgot . . . at least I counted four boys and Tom, so that's good. As the attached photo shows, we have the whole back of the boat to ourselves . . . probably because the darn kitten has been yowling the whole time, leading Sir Puggleton to bark in some kind of cross-species sympathy. Only Zeus is keeping his mouth shut in a wonderful example of feline dignity. Oy.

Anyway, I cannot wait . . . almost five blissful

weeks of beach life! I do admit I'm a little jealous of Tom. August is a great month to be a teacher. Still, I'll play hooky a fair bit—if all else fails I'll tell everyone the Internet connection went out. After all, we are 20 miles out to sea.

Can't wait to see you. Right before Labor Day, yeah? We'll save some sand and sunshine!

Love, your bro

The van had barely stopped moving down the white crushed-shell driveway when Jax and Sam flung open their doors and tumbled out.

"AHHHHH! WE'RE HERE! WE'RE HERE! IT LOOKS EXACTLY THE SAME!" Jax bellowed, running full tilt toward the gray-shingled cottage. Sir Puggleton followed, nose close to the ground as he inhaled all the exciting new smells. Jax inhaled too. It smelled like ocean, and hot sun on grass, and the wild beach roses that grew like crazy all along the fence by the driveway.

"Duh! What were you expecting, that it would somehow turn into a brick apartment building? It's been here for practically a hundred years, moron," Sam said. But he grinned as he grabbed Jax in a headlock. Jax yelped and tackled Sam's knees, sending them both laughing onto the lawn.

The Nugget, as it was named, was an exceedingly knobby house that looked as though each room had been added on without much thought. It looked this way because that was exactly how it had been built, with the original one-room fisherman's shack expanded by different owners until it had reached its current shape. Papa's parents, Mimi and Boppa, had bought it back when Papa and Aunt Lucy were babies. Not terribly much had changed since. Inside was a big kitchen, a small living room, two small bedrooms (one of which was Papa's office), and a sleeping loft with four beds and a ladder to get up and down. There was a bathroom too, of course, off the kitchen. An outdoor shower in a shady wooden stall and a back deck, where rabbits and even deer sometimes wandered, completed the property. It was tiny. And it was often very hot. It was impossible to keep mosquitoes out, as the screens were all crooked. It was, as far as Jax was concerned, a perfect house.

"Nobody goes running off until we unload the car," Papa ordered, his arms full of suitcases and bags of books.

"And somebody better let those cats out before they lose their minds," Dad added. "Make sure Lili has her collar on. We don't want to lose her!" Lili the kitten had never been to Rock Island before, unlike Zeus, who considered it his personal kingdom. The Fletchers had learned to step carefully on the back deck in the morning, as Zeus often left the family a prized mouse head or bit of toad.

Reluctantly the boys returned to the van. Each boy's choice made clear his priorities. Sam grabbed the giant industrial-sized boxes of cereal, peanut butter, and potato chips, stacking them so high he could barely see his way up the path. Eli carefully took out the telescope and microscope, both wrapped in towels, and refused to talk to anyone until he had placed them safely inside on the faded couch. Frog took his nets and collecting buckets and made it as far as the edge of the driveway before he dropped them and started trying to catch grasshoppers. Jax grabbed the mesh bag full of soccer balls, footballs, baseball gloves, and other equipment, then tucked the pop-up soccer nets under his other arm and dragged them toward the wide backyard. Rounding the corner of the house, he looked up and screamed, loud and shrill.

"What's wrong?" Papa yelled, dropping the bags and sprinting toward the backyard, Frog close on his heels. Dad and the rest of Jax's brothers burst through the back door at the same time. Jax barely noticed. The sports equipment lay forgotten at his feet, and all he could do was stare.

In front of him, as expected, was the large backyard, bordered by bushes and tall grass with a winding, barely visible path through it. Like the rest of the island, everything was low and scrubby, trees battered and bent by ocean winds, the sandy soil refusing to let anything but the most determined grass and wildflowers grow. The tall grass—and the path, which had been created by years of Fletchers running back and forth—separated the Nugget from the Rock Island lighthouse. But now this! The path was abruptly cut off by a giant chain-link fence. The fence surrounded the lighthouse, looming large and hideous over the backyard and blocking the Fletchers from the place they all considered part of their home. What was going on? For as long as the Fletchers could remember the lighthouse had been ignored, and they had been free to climb the winding staircase and bring binoculars to the top and look for seals. And now this . . . this . . . this *menace*. Jax felt a sick swooping feeling in his stomach. Who would have done this?

"Good Lord, Jackson, unless something's on fire—like one of your brothers—don't shriek like that," Papa said, one hand on his chest. "You don't scream bloody murder unless it's an emergency."

"This IS an emergency!" Jax said hotly. Didn't his fathers see this thing in front of them? "What the heck is going on? Why can't we go to the lighthouse?"

"Huh. That's weird," Papa said, staring up. "That's definitely weird."

"There's a Keep Out sign," Sam said. He had walked the path as far as it would go, and stood up against the fence. Even though he was nearly Dad's height, he looked small and insignificant against the tall metal grid.

"Jason, you haven't heard anything about the lighthouse being closed, have you?" Dad asked.

Papa shook his head, his eyes hidden behind sunglasses. But Jax could tell by the way his mouth was shut tight that Papa didn't like the fence any more than he did.

"Well, clearly we need to get some information. But let's not panic, guys," Dad said, walking up to join Sam. "Could just be that the town was doing some repairs, or even painting it. Right? There's probably a really simple explanation."

He said the last words to Papa, as though Papa were the one he was really telling not to panic.

They all gazed up at the lighthouse. It looked just the same as always: white and round and enormous, with a thick red stripe around the middle. The paint was faded, Jax supposed, and he could see it chipping in a few places. But who cared? What if it didn't reopen for weeks? They only had a month on the island.

Slowly, the family walked around the fence. When they got to the front of it, a giant chain held the gate shut. Jax stared, then closed his eyes; surely he was seeing it wrong. On the fence, next to another Keep Out sign, was a sign that said FOR SALE: CONTACT TOWN CLERK. And below it hung a smaller sign that simply said Sale Pending.

Jax turned and kicked a rock as hard as he could. He kicked another, even though it hurt his toes. His eyes were hot and itchy and he almost felt like he could cry.

"What does *pending* mean?" Frog asked.

"It means that someone's going to buy it. Buy the lighthouse," said Sam, sounding numb. "But how can they do that? How can it be for sale?"

Papa, who had been staring at the sign, finally turned away, shaking himself slightly. He smiled at the boys, but it looked forced. "Sometimes lighthouses are bought by public groups that promise to take good care of them," he said, and his voice was the too-bright cheerful voice he used when on difficult work calls. "Maybe it's just something like that." He started to walk back toward the Nugget. Fast.

The boys stared at the lighthouse for a second longer before following.

"I'll call Captain Jim later and get the scoop, okay, Jax?" Papa said over his shoulder. Captain Jim was one of the few people who lived on Rock Island all year long, and he knew everything. "As Dad said, let's not panic. There might be a simple explanation. So why don't we finish unpacking, and maybe we'll have time for a quick swim. Sound good?"

Jax glanced at his brothers. They looked how he felt, unsure about what to do without the lighthouse offering its usual welcome. Eli finally stepped forward.

"Come on, Jax, let's do Rock, Paper, Scissors for the window bed," he said. The two of them always fought over the bed by the window, which had the lowest headroom but the most interesting view.

Jax nodded and walked with Eli back toward the house, following Papa's retreating form. Dad, Frog, and Sam followed.

"Will they do construction on the lighthouse?" Frog asked. "That looks like the fence they put around construction sites. That would be neat if there were diggers and backhoes here."

Jax couldn't help scowling at Frog. "We don't want backhoes and diggers. We want to get in the lighthouse!"

Frog's smile dimmed and he slid his hand into Dad's. Jax felt even worse. This wasn't exactly the return to Rock Island he had been dreaming of.

Later, once the car was unloaded, once his paper had beaten Eli's rock, once they'd set up the soccer nets and started playing, Jax felt better. At least, as long as he didn't look at the chain-link fence. When they played soccer he made sure he was shooting toward the far goal so he could keep his back to the monstrosity that was ruining his island.

Finally, sweaty and thirsty, the boys flung themselves onto the deck chairs and panted like Sir Puggleton after a long romp.

"Do we have lemonade?" Sam asked.

"No, nobody's gone to Mr. Hooper's yet," Eli said. Hooper's Grocery was the only real store on the island.

It was all the way on the other side, six miles away on the slow, winding road that snaked down the island's center.

"What about Popsicles?" Jax asked. He was hanging his head off the edge of the chair, enjoying the sensation of dizziness that being upside down brought.

"No. Nobody's been to the store," Eli said again.

"Do we have ice cream?" Frog said eagerly, popping up. "Oooh! I want ice cream!"

"Nobody's been to the store!" Eli said, annoyed. "Do you think we could pack it in our bags? There's no ice cream, no Popsicles, and no—"

He paused. Jax lifted his head. In the distance came a sound, a sound they knew perfectly well but had never heard on Rock Island in all the years of Fletcher life.

"Is that . . . ," Jax began.

Sir Puggleton began to bark, his loud, I-Am-Making-an-Announcement bark.

"ICE CREAM TRUCK! ICE CREAM TRUUUUUCK!" Frog made a noise that was between a scream and a gurgle as he ran around in maniacal circles. "It's here! There's an ice cream truck here! ICE CREAM TRUUUUUUUUUUCK!" With a final piercing scream pitched so high it could have been heard by bats, he disappeared around the side of the house.

The rest of the Fletchers followed on his heels. An ice cream truck on Rock Island? Who could have imagined such a thing? They had them back home in Shipton, of course. In fact, the truck would come to their street and patiently wait while Frog sounded the alarm so loudly that any kid within two blocks knew about it. Frog was, Jax thought as he ran toward the truck, a kind of ice cream truck groupie. Soon he'd be asking for the driver's autograph.

By the time the boys corralled their fathers and made it to the street, the truck was a few houses away, but moving slowly. As they ran behind it, it stopped, right in front of the old Wheelright house. Unlike the rest of the cottages, this was a sea captain's house, enormous and proud. But it had sat empty for ages, longer than any of the Fletcher boys could remember. Apparently some rich people who lived overseas owned it and never bothered to visit. Now, it seemed, they had come back.

Quickly the Fletchers circled the window of the ice cream truck and shouted out their requests, tacking on a "please" and "thank you" when Dad caught their eyes.

"Oooh, are you the Fletchers? Val's parents said that *boys* were arriving today, and here you are!"

The voice, and the person it was attached to, distracted all the boys but Frog from the ice cream. (Frog, of course, had secured his chocolate-Oreo-crunch bar and was wolfing it down with gusto.) They saw a girl, teenage-ish, leaning confidently against the imposing fence of the Wheelright house. Jax, in his head at least, groaned loudly and fake-barfed. Some girls were totally fine. Olivia, who played soccer and lived nearby, was fine. So was Dylan from his class, who played ice hockey, and Kate, whose mother was a marine biologist and who had swum with manta rays and dolphins. Even Sam's friend Emily Shawble, who had convinced Sam to do the school play last year, was pretty funny and cool. But this girl, Jax thought, seemed like the worst kind of girl. She had on a puffy short skirt and sparkly sandals and big stupid sunglasses that practically hid her whole face.

"They didn't say *cute* boys, though, did they, Val?" she continued.

Jax looked around. There was a second girl, wearing some crazy wraparound-dress thing and mirrored sunglasses. She also had a big floppy hat on that hid most of her face, and even weirder, she was holding her phone up as though filming them. Jax felt his face getting hot. But the first girl wasn't looking at him. She was looking right at Sam. The girl in the crazy wraparound thing pressed something on her phone and put it down, then spoke.

"Hey there! I'm Valerie Galindo—Val for short—and this is my friend Janie. She's here for the week."

The other girl, Janie, pushed forward from the fence and held out her hand, as though expecting them to shake it. "Awesome to meet you," she said, peering over her sunglasses.

But Sam had already started in on his two-handed Bomb Pop–and–strawberry shortcake combo, and Jax was dealing with a melting Klondike bar. While the girl had been talking Frog had simply walked away, and Eli, probably sensing escape, followed, slurping the edges of his rainbow snow cone. It was just Jax and Sam. Jax stared at his brother.

"Hey," Sam said finally, with a jerk of his chin. "I'm Sam. That's my brother Jax. See you around." He wheeled and started to walk back to the Nugget.

Jax hurried to catch up. As he ran, he saw another kid, younger than the fluffy girls, crouching on the edge of the road, where the pavement turned to dirt. Whoever it was had a Chicago ball cap pulled down low, filthy cutoff shorts, and a bug box that was shaking with the movement of whatever was inside. Jax paused for a moment to watch.

"Snake," the kid said quietly, not looking up at Jax. "Just a garter."

Jax nodded. "Cool," he said, then kept moving to catch up with his brother.

"What was that?" he asked Sam, who had finished both his ice creams and was looking a bit wistful. "Those girls were so weird. And that one . . . Val . . . why was she taking a video of us? What the heck?" Jax didn't say what he really felt, which was that the weirdest part was them calling Sam "cute." He was afraid Sam might punch him if he brought it up. But Sam only shrugged.

"Whatever. Weird girls are weird. I'll tell you something

more interesting, though. The fact that an ice cream truck comes down this road is epic. That's what my English teacher would call a pivotal turning point in the summer. Ice cream every day—maybe twice a day! Epic." Sam stared off into space, presumably imagining a life where the ice cream truck remained parked outside the house and he never ran out of allowance.

Jax agreed, and then, since they had caught up to the others, the boys all had to listen to Frog sing his special ice cream truck song again and again until Jax threatened to gag him with his dirty sweat sock. And so they tumbled back to the Nugget, loud and laughing. The sun was low and warm in the sky, and the breeze had picked up, rustling and shivering the tall grass so that it looked like rippling water. The smell of the sea was stronger now, and Jax couldn't wait to head to the beach. He was almost perfectly happy, at least until he looked out past the back deck. Tomorrow they would learn what was going on with their lighthouse. Maybe Dad was right. Maybe it was just some boring grown-up tax thing or something. For today, he might as well enjoy everything that was still perfect about Rock Island.

Chapter Three

IN WHICH SAM THINKS THE NEIGHBORHOOD IS GOING DOWNHILL

August 3, 10:36 a.m.
Yo Em! We got here two days ago, and it's cool to be back but we're SO crowded. 4 in a room and the freaking cat snores so loud I can't sleep. R U in rehearsals yet?

"Sam! Are you coming? We're leaving, with or without you!" Dad called from the driveway.

The family had more or less settled in, though for the boys unpacking meant dumping their duffel bags into the corner of the sleeping loft and digging through them as needed. They had made the ceremonial first trip to Hooper's Market, and they'd seen Mimi and Boppa's friends the Gootkinds and the Levees, who always exclaimed over how big they were. But they hadn't gotten any answers about the lighthouse. It sat painfully out of reach, the ugly metal fence as daunting as ever. Still, the first full day, and the campfire last night, had been wonderful. They'd lain out on the blanket as the fire died, staring up at the crazy-bright stars and talking about everything they would do on the island.

Now the family was in the driveway, preparing to head to the rocky cove beach right near the house. The bigger beach, with its wide sandy dunes and rolling surf, was farther away and required a car ride (or a long bike ride), but the cove was around the corner, close enough for the boys to walk without a grown-up and look for crabs and the occasional sea star, if Sam swore on his life that he wouldn't let anyone swim. But today Dad was coming with them so they could all swim and hang out while Papa finished his work calls. Then, when Papa was done, they could go to the real beach, as Sam called it. He was hoping he could bring his surfboard and get some rides if the waves weren't too crazy.

"SAM!" Dad's voice floated up into the loft again, louder this time.

Sam pressed the Off button on his phone and threw it on his bed. He wasn't really surprised that Em hadn't texted back. She was probably in rehearsal for the summer show. The Shipton Community Theatre was doing a bunch of wacky fairy tales, and Em had the lead in practically half of them. She'd begged Sam to try out too, but since he was away for the month of August it wasn't really an option. Not that he was sure he wanted to, anyway, but still. Maybe it would have been cool.

With one last look at his silent phone, Sam headed down the ladder and outside to meet his family.

"I'm coming. Chill out," he said, grabbing the crabbing net and starting to walk while dribbling a soccer ball along the road. "Jax, you up for a pass? Get ready!" The sun and salt smell worked its magic, and Sam grinned, ready to forget his phone and everything else on the mainland.

Frog raced to catch up. "I've got my net too! And we're going to look for Gar Baby, right? I'll recognize him, I think. He had an unusual shell. I hope he knows me! Do you think he will?" His brown paw slipped into Sam's and Sam squeezed it.

"Who knows, Froggie? You're pretty hard to forget."

Frog beamed. "That's what I think too," he said, and jumped a little as they walked.

Behind them, Jax and Eli were talking while passing the ball back and forth.

"It's not that big a deal! I don't know why you won't just try it. Papa said if you were up to it this would be our year!"

Sam could tell from Eli's silence that his brother was probably scowling down at the dirt road. Finally Eli spoke.

"I have tried it. I—"

"That was two years ago! You were a baby then. You—"

"*I'm* not a baby!" Frog interrupted. "And I'm six-almost-seven."

Both Jax and Eli ignored this.

"You're almost eleven. Come ON. You're ruining it for the rest of us," Jax kept going, his voice rising in annoyance.

Sam knew, of course, what this was about. There were several tiny uninhabited islands off the coast of Rock Island, and it was possible to kayak out to them, if one was a fairly steady and intrepid kayaker. Eli was neither. But that didn't stop Jax from nagging him to try. Papa had talked about an all-family excursion to Tuckernocket, the farthest island, and the one most likely to be visited by seals. Papa had said that Eli didn't have to do it if he didn't want, but the thought of his brother staying home was too much for Jax.

Before Eli could answer they rounded the bend in the dirt road that led to the cove. There was one mangy Jeep in the parking area that they all recognized as belonging to one of their neighbors. Other than that, it was empty.

"Let's find Gar Baby!" Frog cried, letting go of Sam's hand and flying down the rocks toward the shore.

The rest of them followed, and soon they were all wading in the chilly cove water, heads down, eyes peeled for fish, green crabs, and yes, hermit crabs.

"I think this is him! Oh, wait, never mind, this one's smaller," Frog said, picking up, then discarding a tiny hermit crab.

Sam moved back toward the shoreline, where a small strip of sand made for a nice break from the rocks.

"Want me to dig you a swimming pool?" he asked Frog. "We can make a big one!"

The others rushed over, eager to help, and before long Sam was in the center of a massive hole, wet sand stuck to his legs, arms windmilling as he flung handfuls of it to the side.

"Build up that wall," he called to Jax. "It's going to need protection as the tide comes in."

Frog got in the hole with Sam, while Eli ran back and forth for rocks to make a fence. They were deep into the construction when a babble of voices startled them. Sam looked up from the pool, where Frog was letting the wet sand trickle through his fingers into towers and spires along Sam's shoulders and knees, covering him with dribble castles.

Walking down the path were the girls from yesterday. They were armed with chairs, a waterproof music player blasting some pop song, and a small cooler. Behind them was the kid who'd had the snake, wearing the same green and orange board shorts as Jax.

"Oh, hey! The Fletcher boys are here! *¡Hola, chicos! ¿Cómo está el agua hoy?*" the one in front said. She—

Sam thought her name was Val, but he wasn't sure—was wearing a long, fancy-looking white skirt and a kind of graffitied tank top in a neon orange so bright it almost vibrated in the sun.

Sam gave her a blank stare. He had no idea what she was saying, and her shirt hurt his eyes.

"Do you guys speak Spanish?" the girl asked. "Just asking how the water is." She adjusted her bug-eye sunglasses and smiled. "Now, smile and wave," she instructed, lifting her phone again. "Got to get a good panoramic shot of the beach!"

Janie caught up to her. "God, you are so *obsessed* with that video camera," she said. "Can't you give it a rest for ten seconds?" Before Val could answer, Janie caught sight of Sam. "Oooh! So *cute* that you're playing with your little brothers! Don't you think, Val? Isn't it cute?"

Sam turned his back to them, his face blazing. There was literally nothing he could imagine worse than being called cute by a girl like Janie.

The girls dropped their gear a short ways up the beach from Sam's swimming pool, pulled off their clothes, and set up their chairs, laying them flat for sunbathing.

Dad looked up from his book, frowned a little, and then glanced at the music player, which was playing a Spanish pop song.

"Hey, girls, any chance you could leave the music at home or use earphones? We kind of like the quiet."

At that moment Eli shrieked loud enough to be heard on the mainland as Jax poured a bucket of water over him. Frog screamed with laughter.

"Well, not quiet, exactly. But still," Dad said.

Sam closed his eyes in embarrassment.

"Oh! Sure! Sorry about that," Val said, and though her voice was polite, Sam thought she sounded like she was trying not to laugh.

"Do you want help with your sand castle? It's adorable," Janie said, wandering over. She was paler and skinnier than Val, and wore an even stupider bathing suit, complete with ruffles and no straps.

Sam flushed. He pushed Frog's hand away and stood up, dripping sand and salt water from shoulder to feet. Stepping over the rock wall, he headed down to the water to rinse off.

"Hey! Those were my dribble castles. Come back!" Frog called, but Sam ignored him.

He dove under the water, enjoying the shock of cold and the sweeping feeling of the sand washing off his sticky body. He wished he could stay under there, away from his embarrassing dad and the girls who seemed intent on ruining his summer. But of course he needed to breathe. Coming to the surface, he floated on his back, staring at the sky.

Jax and Eli swam over. Jax dove and resurfaced a few feet away, where the water was a little shallower. "Want to throw the football?" he asked.

Sam nodded. They might as well. The beach was taken over by twits, or so it seemed.

They did Rock, Paper, Scissors, and Sam lost, so he swam in to get the football.

As he passed Frog on the shore, his brother looked up. “I think I found him! See? Doesn’t he look like Gar Baby?” he asked, holding up a crab.

Sam glanced down, then over at Janie, who was propped on her elbows, watching him. He shrugged. “Maybe. Whatever.” He kept walking and grabbed the football, pivoting and heading back to the water without looking at the girls.

Frog, undeterred by Sam’s lack of enthusiasm, was talking quietly to the crab. “Hello, Gar Baby, my old friend. Would you like to come home and watch a movie with me?”

Sam rolled his eyes. Hopefully the girls were far enough away that they couldn’t hear Frog. But judging by the giggles floating down behind him, it seemed unlikely.

As Sam reached the water he looked over to where the younger kid was crouched, eyes glued to the football in Sam’s hands.

Sam paused. “What’s your name?” he asked.

“Alex,” the kid said, smiling a little.

“I’m Sam. Those are my brothers Jax and Eli out there. Want to play football with us? Two on a side,” Sam said. He didn’t really know why he asked. The kid just looked so forlorn, sitting alone in the wet sand.

"Sure!" Alex jumped up and followed Sam into the water.

Within minutes they had started a two-per-side game, with Sam and Eli trying to score by getting the football to shore, while Jax and Alex aimed for a jutting outcrop of rock. So far Jax and the new kid were winning.

"ALEX! Come ON. We've got to go get ready for lunch. Mami has guests coming!" Val was yelling from the shore.

Alex looked disgusted. "Gotta go. You going to be here tomorrow?"

Jax looked at Sam.

Sam shrugged. "No idea. We might go to Surf Beach." He wasn't sure he wanted anyone related to the girls continuing to hang out with them, but Jax interrupted.

"Sure. We'll try to come back in the morning. Meet you here!"

Alex nodded, and with a series of arguments over who had to carry the cooler and who was in charge of the chairs, Alex and the girls were gone.

The Fletchers were once again alone at the cove, but it didn't feel the same. Sam sighed and dove under the water. Somehow, it still didn't feel quite like they had arrived.

Chapter Four

IN WHICH FROG DECIDES TO BE AN ANIMAL TRAINER

> "According to animal scientists, cats evolved from water creatures later than many other mammals. The common myth that cats hate water is largely not borne out by fact, and most cats are adept swimmers."
>
> *Facts About Cats for Young Readers,* by I. M. Ferrie

The first few days on the island were awesome, by Frog's standards. They had gotten to go to the big beach, and Frog was now old enough to jump or dive in the waves with Dad or Sam or Papa, and sometimes he even tried to ride them, if they weren't too rough. And at Cove Beach he could paddle for hours, until he got so cold that he couldn't stop shaking.

"I'm shivering for fun!" he'd tried protesting to Dad,

who had ordered him out of the water. “I’m not really c-c-cold! It’s just a game!”

But Dad hadn’t believed him, and Frog spent the rest of the afternoon wrapped in towels trying to warm up.

They had even gone to the tiny Rock Island library, where Frog had his own library card. So far, except for the lighthouse, everything was perfect.

Then, just as they were deciding whether to ride their bikes to see if the blackberries were out yet or to go to the beach, the rain clouds came.

It had been raining for only a few hours, but it felt much longer. Frog, who didn’t like loud noises, had heard Dad tell Papa that there might be thunderstorms, and he had been in a state of high alert ever since.

“Is it going to be a thunder, Dad? Is it? IS THAT THUNDER?” Frog bellowed, climbing into Dad’s lap on the couch.

“No, Froggie, it’s just Eli and Jax chasing each other in the loft. Boys! Knock it off! You really can’t run up there—it’s like a herd of elephants overhead!” Dad yelled, but the footsteps didn’t stop.

“Let’s read a book, okay, buddy? I don’t think there’s going to be a thunderstorm. I think it’s going to stop raining any minute now,” Dad said, pulling Frog’s head out of the cushions and grabbing the stack of books from the floor. "Do you want to read this one about cats?"

Frog agreed, and soon they were deep into the habits and habitats of domestic and wild felines. As though to show off the species, Zeus strutted into the room and paraded across the couch, waving his tail in their faces.

"Dad! Did you read this part?" Frog looked up. "It says cats can actually swim really well. Do you think our cats can?"

Dad, who had picked up a magazine when Frog started reading to himself, answered absently. "Probably, buddy."

"Really? You really do? Can we try?" Frog was excited. He forgot about the thunder and even his brothers stomping overhead. That would be really neat, to teach Zeus to swim. Sir Puggleton wasn't much of a swimmer, and Frog had always wanted a pet that could swim with him, just like the big dogs swimming at the beach.

"Hmm? Sure, Frog-o. I'm sure that's fine," Dad said, still not looking up.

Frog dropped the book back on the pile and stared at Zeus, transfixed by the thought of his new swimming companion. How best to start? He considered carefully. It was probably not a good idea to bring Zeus to the beach right away. After all, *he* hadn't started in the ocean! He'd started . . . Of course! Frog stood up.

"Come on, Zeus. We're going on an adventure," Frog said, grabbing the huge beast around the middle. Zeus's legs dangled below Frog's skinny arms, and Frog couldn't help lurching a little under the weight.

"How much does Zeus *weigh*?" he asked, huffing.

Sam didn't look up from his phone. He had found that if he stood in the kitchen near the window the phone might let him send and receive texts.

"He weighed eighteen pounds when he went to the vet this spring. They want us to put him on a diet."

Frog made it to the bathroom and, a little faster than he had meant to, dropped Zeus to the floor. Zeus meowed reproachfully.

"Stay here," Frog said, and dashed back to the kitchen for cat treats. When he got back to the bathroom, Zeus had leapt onto the back of the toilet and was staring at him.

Frog gave him a treat, thinking about the sea lions at the zoo and the trainers who gave them fish. He felt very grown-up and important, training a cat like this. "Good Zeus," he said proudly. The training was going well so far.

Carefully, Frog turned on the water in the old stained bathtub, making sure it wasn't too cold or too hot. Dropping the plug into the tub, he stared doubtfully at the rising water. How much was the right amount? He needed Zeus to be able to paddle, and not sink. Zeus yowled at the door, but Frog the trainer was ready. He gave the cat another treat and patted his head.

Soon the tub was full, and Frog shut off the faucets.

Without the racket of the running water he could hear his brothers shouting over who got to be the race car in Monopoly. Frog shook his head—his brothers were acting so babyish while he, Frog, was training an animal. He took a bunch of treats and placed them carefully on the floor where he could reach them.

Then he grabbed Zeus. "I think you're going to really like this!" he said brightly. "I know it might be a little scary at first, but don't worry. Cats are natural swimmers."

He lowered Zeus toward the water. The cat tensed in his hands, but Frog, kneeling over the tub, was steady. He had just put Zeus's paws in the water when the door swung open, banging into the wall with a loud thunk.

"Who's in here? What . . . HEY! WHAT ARE YOU DOING?" Jax yelled.

"AAAAH!" With a shout of surprise, Frog dropped Zeus.

There was a splash, then a second of silence as Zeus disappeared under the water. But then he emerged.

"YOOOOOWWWRRRRLLLBBRRAAAZZZZLLEEE!"

The noise coming out of Zeus was terrifying, a combination howl, yowl, and low, deep moan that Frog had never heard before. With a mighty leap, Zeus sprang out of the tub, the strange, unearthly noise still emerging from his throat.

"What the heck did you do?" Jax screamed, as Zeus flung himself against Jax's legs, madly pawing at him to get past. "Hey! Get OFF!"

Zeus, who had somehow gotten tangled in Jax's legs, pushed off hard and raced, still caterwauling, out of the bathroom.

Dad, Sam, and Eli ran in. The tiny bathroom, which barely fit the tub, toilet, and sink, was hot, flooded, and very, very crowded.

"Jax? Why are you yelling? What's going on?" Dad said.

Papa ran in before Frog could answer. "What happened? Why is Zeus soaking wet?" He looked at Jax. "And what the heck happened to you?"

Jax was on the floor, clutching his ankle. "That beast attacked me! Look at this! I've got like ten cuts! Why is it always me? WHY?"

Everyone was babbling, describing the noises coming out of Zeus, asking Jax what he had done, interrupting each other and arguing, until Jax bellowed, "I DIDN'T DO ANYTHING! Why does everyone think it was me? It was Frog!"

Everyone turned and stared at Frog. He looked down. Beneath him, the cat treats were dissolving in the puddles of water, turning to brown goop. He blinked back tears. Jax had scared him, that was all! He had been startled, and dropped Zeus, and it had all gone bad.

Papa shoved through the rest of the boys. "Why don't you guys clear out? Tom, you want to see if you can find a Band-Aid—or a few Band-Aids—for Jax?"

Slowly the bathroom emptied. Frog kept staring at the mushy cat treats. Outside the room, he could hear his brothers shouting as they tried to grab Zeus and dry him off.

"Hey, bud? What was that all about?" Papa's voice was soft, but Frog still didn't look up.

He shrugged.

"Did you mean to drop Zeus in the bathtub? Or was it . . ." Papa paused for a second, obviously trying to think of a scenario where Frog would have accidentally been holding the enormous cat over the tub.

"I didn't mean to drop him!" Frog burst out. "I was going to lower him gently." He pressed his lips together. He didn't want to explain to Papa what he was doing. He remembered how good it felt to be an animal trainer, and a small sob escaped. If Jax hadn't come in and scared him, it would have all worked perfectly.

Papa's arms came around him until he was wrapped up in a full hug.

"Hey! You're not in trouble. Well, not in big trouble, certainly. Why don't you tell me why you were gently lowering Zeus into the tub?"

Frog's voice was muffled in Papa's soft shirt. "I was teaching Zeus to swim. I read about it in a library book. And I asked Dad—"

Papa started to say something, then cut himself off. "Okay. Good. Go on," he said, his voice encouraging.

"Well, that's it. I was just . . . I wanted him to swim because according to my book, cats are natural swimmers, and maybe he'd really like it. And maybe sometime when he got used to it he would come with us and swim in the ocean. He would be my swimming buddy." Frog's voice got stronger as he talked. "And we could do that, Papa, couldn't we? I mean, I can try again! I think Zeus was just startled, is all." He sniffled loudly.

Before Papa could answer, Eli burst in. "The sun is out and we're packing up for the beach. Come on!" He ran back out again without waiting for an answer.

Frog looked up at Papa and smiled. "It didn't thunder!" he said. "Let's go to the beach."

Papa smiled back and squeezed him. "Sounds good. But hey, buddy? About Zeus . . . ," he started.

Frog paused on his way out the door. "Don't worry, Papa! I'll tell everyone before I train him again," he said. He felt *much* better. Next time Zeus would love the water. He was sure of it.

Chapter Five

IN WHICH THE PROBLEM OF THE LIGHTHOUSE IS EXPLAINED, BUT JAX WOULD LIKE TO SHOOT THE MESSENGER

August 7
To: LucyCupcake
From: PapaBear
Subject: Lighthouse
Dear Luce—

Well, I'm not going to lie, it's really weird having the lighthouse closed up and off-limits. I'm having a hard time getting any answers, other than that the town started to explore the idea of selling it in order to pay for some upcoming improvements, and then someone was injured on-site. But whether the buyers are a public land trust who will keep it just the same, or have other plans, I can't seem to find out.

Honestly, Lucy, I know it isn't really ours, but that lighthouse always felt like part of our own personal island. It sure is a part of our history here. I mean, how many spitting contests did we have from the balcony?

And that's where Tom and I decided to adopt Sam, all those many years ago. I still remember standing up there, staring out at the ocean, trying to imagine what it would mean to bring our son here someday. It was the most exhilarating and terrifying feeling. And the next year we brought one-year-old Sam up there . . .

Well. Enough of my sentimental whining. Maybe we'll find out that the fence is temporary and everything will go back to the way it was. Here's hoping.

Love, your bro

"ICE CREEEAAAAM!" Frog yelled, and Jax dropped the wet towels he was hanging up on the clothesline.

The truck had, after a whispered consultation between the driver and Papa, stopped coming every day, and now its arrival sent Frog into a new frenzy each time. Jax had to admit, it *was* pretty amazing to have an ice cream truck on their road in Rock Island. The only problem was that it always stopped halfway between their house and the old Wheelright house, which meant they would run into video-crazy Valerie and her stupid friend every time. Janie had stayed on an extra few days, apparently to stare at Sam and turn him into a grouch-zombie who refused to look at anyone.

Still, Alex seemed pretty cool. The few times they'd been at Cove Beach together, Jax and Alex had thrown the football and once even caught a small lobster that was stuck under the rocks. Sadly, Jax was extra glad to have someone else to hang out with, as Sam seemed intent on being alone these days and Eli was still sulking over the kayak thing. Never before had the Fletcher boys needed additional friends on Rock Island, but this year, that, like so much else, was different.

They still, after one whole week on the island, hadn't solved the mystery of the lighthouse. Captain Jim Fish had been busy, out fishing most days, and only told Papa that the town had decided to sell the lighthouse because there was some structural damage. They had hoped a group would come along and fix it, like a preservation group or a museum or something. But a buyer was interested, and then got hurt at the site, so now the town had to address the problem right away. Jax didn't really understand it at all. Still, they were going back into town today, and he hoped they'd finally get some answers.

Meanwhile there was ice cream. He ran outside after his brothers, groaning a little at the thought of the girls giggling and trying to talk to Sam, who would no doubt be doing his grouch-zombie routine. He ran back into the house to grab his net: Alex had said there was a nest of tiny green snakes somewhere behind their house, and Jax was desperate to catch one.

“Coming?” he asked Eli, who was standing, unmoving, in the yard.

“Yeah. I’m just . . .” He trailed off.

Jax didn’t bother to ask him what he was doing. Eli had been gazing toward the lighthouse, still untouched and abandoned.

He punched Eli’s arm, but gently. “I know. We’ll find out in town today. Who knows? Maybe it’s nothing. Maybe by tomorrow we’ll be back in!” Jax tried to sound positive, but he was worried. Nobody had been at the lighthouse to paint or fix stuff or anything. It was the same as always, except for the terrible fence keeping them out. And who knows what the new owners would do. Maybe they’d keep it open. But what if they didn’t?

As the boys walked toward the ice cream truck, Jax was surprised to see grown-ups standing with the Galindo kids and stupid Janie. He had never seen Alex’s parents—usually the three would come to Cove Beach by themselves, or occasionally they’d get driven to Surf Beach by a babysitter who stayed under an umbrella and read.

Now Alex was standing with a tall woman in a giant straw hat and a T-shirt that read COFFEE: POWER UP, with a picture of a coffee mug plugged into an outlet. She looked a little like Valerie, and Alex too, Jax guessed, though mostly it was the long hair and the bug-eye sunglasses that made the mother and daughter look alike. A tall skinny white guy with a scruffy beard and a pair of ripped shorts was paying for the ice cream. He looked over as the Fletchers walked up to the truck window.

"Ah! You must be the famous Fletcher boys! Nice to meet you! Now, don't tell me . . . you're Sam, right?" he said, shaking hands with Frog.

Frog giggled. "No!"

"Well then, you must be Jax. My kids told me Jax was really cool and liked to play football. That's you, right?" the man said, squinting and looking confused.

Frog laughed harder and the man clapped him on the back. "I know, I know. You're Frog. And that tall fellow is Sam, and I think I recognize the rest of you too. What can I get you? Ice cream is on me."

The boys looked at one another, good manners warring with greed. Frog spoke first.

"Well, you're not a stranger, since you're Alex and Valerie's dad, right?"

The man nodded solemnly. "Sorry. I should have introduced myself. John Galindo-Green. I met your parents yesterday, and I think they wouldn't mind if we subsidize your ice cream habit just this once."

Frog paused. "Does *subsidize* mean 'buy it'? Because if it does I want a double-dip chocolate Bomb Pop. But if it doesn't I only have a dollar and I'll get a grape Popsicle."

John Galindo-Green laughed out loud. "It does indeed mean to buy it! I'm a writer, and sometimes we use a long, slippery word when a short one will do just fine. Thanks for reminding me. Now let's get you boys your ice cream."

Soon everyone was served, and while Sam edged back to the house, Jax and Eli wandered around the back of the massive mansion with Alex, hoping to see the green snakes. Just as they were peering under an old rubber tire that was lying on the far end of the property, a voice pierced the quiet.

"Aleeex! Where are you? We're going on a bike ride!"

Alex groaned and stood up. "Well, that's it for the snakes. They disappear when there's the slightest bit of noise. And with my sister there's always more than a little bit of noise. . . . It's like an explosion. Especially when her friends are around."

Jax and Eli both kept quiet. Neither one wanted to say anything nasty about their friend's sister, but Jax had to bite his tongue not to agree. Instead he gazed away from the tire and back across the windswept moors, toward their house. In the distance he could see the lighthouse, large and important, against the deep blue sky. From here you could barely see the fence.

He turned to Alex. "Hey! Do *you* know what's going on with the lighthouse? We used to be able to go there all the time and now there's a fence around it."

Eli chimed in. "It was amazing," he said, his voice wistful. "It's right outside our back deck, and we would have water fights, and see the seals on Tuckernocket from the top—"

"—which we could go kayaking to if you weren't such a wimp!" Jax interrupted, annoyed all over again at his brother.

"—and we even slept upstairs there once. Well, most of the night, until midnight at least," Eli continued, ignoring him. "And now there's a terrible fence around it, and we can't even get in!"

Alex looked impressed. "That sounds so cool. I wish I could do that! All I know—"

Valerie's voice cut in. "*There* you are! I've been calling you. It's Janie's last day, and Mami and Dad want to bike to Gilly's for chowder."

Jax was getting desperate. "Do you know about the lighthouse? Why is the fence there? What's going on?"

Valerie's eyebrows shot up above her silly sunglasses. "Oh! I heard about that! First of all, the federal government is selling it. Did you know they sell a lot of lighthouses? Dad was fascinated and started writing an article about it, so he told us all about it. . . . I guess there are tons of lighthouses, all around the country, that the government just sells off. Whoever buys it has to keep it as a working lighthouse . . . that's part of the deal. Anyway, this one needs some work, and a group of people in town were going to buy it. There are big cracks in the plaster and the town thought it was just cosmetic—you know, that it was just how it looked and not a big problem. Then some artist decided *he* wanted it and put in an offer, but then he was painting up there and got hit with crumbling rock and plaster. I think he was hurt pretty bad! It was big news. It just happened too—a few days before we got here, and we only arrived a week before you guys."

Jax and Eli both digested this in silence. Valerie pushed her sunglasses on top of her head and continued to talk. "I wish we had seen it! I mean, not like I wanted anything bad to happen to him, but it would have been so cool if I had grabbed it on video! It's a cute island, but there's not a lot to do here, really. I joined the theater group, which they were pretty psyched about, since I'll film the play later this month. But other than that . . ." She sighed.

Alex groaned. "She's obsessed with her stupid video camera. She thinks she's going to be the next—"

"The next Sofia Coppola, only the coolest female movie producer in the world," Valerie said, with a roll of her eyes. "And it's better than *you*. What do you want to be, the next—"

"I'm going to be the next Lionel Messi. Only the best soccer player ever," Alex said.

Jax nodded in approval. Messi wasn't *his* favorite soccer player, but it was a solid choice.

"Anyway, she's forever filming everyone and everything. It's totally creepy. Remember that guy who got really mad last summer in Prague? And Mami had to assure him you weren't working for the CIA." Alex sighed. "Anyway, I guess they put a fence around the lighthouse to fix it, or until the new owners take it over or something."

Eli looked concerned. "But there's no work going on. No restoration, no signs about it, just a big Keep Out sign. How long ago did the guy get hurt?"

Valerie answered immediately. "July twenty-fifth. Three days after we got here. I was over at the docks, filming the fishing boats coming in."

"Like watching paint dry," Alex muttered, but Valerie paid no attention.

"*¡Vámanos!*" she said, turning to leave. "Mami will lose her mind if we don't *get moving*!"

Jax and Eli followed them, but Jax's thoughts were still on the lighthouse. He was sorry to hear about the artist, of course. But what was going to happen next? When would they be allowed in their favorite place?

Chapter Six

IN WHICH ELI IS OFFERED A CHALLENGE AND ALL MIGHT BE LOST

Dear Eli: Thanks for your letter. Life on Two Kids Farm is pretty good. . . . We have visitors from Europe staying with us to check out the goats. They brought the most amazing chocolates. Anyway, I'm sending a few photos of Benji with his most recent stitches, and one of the new kittens. Have you found out any news about your lighthouse? I hope you get in there soon. . . . It sounds like it isn't really summer without it.

Love, Anna Bean

It was grocery day, and it was overcast, which meant that the boys all decided to go to town with Dad to get food. Dad had looked a little depressed about it, asking if they were sure they didn't want to play soccer in the yard instead, but they were insistent. Behind his back, Papa pretended to do a victory dance, then waved goodbye.

Eli was torn. Normally they'd never waste an afternoon shopping, but they were cramped at the house, and grouchy. Papa had to take work calls, so they needed to stay quiet, which normally meant they'd go to the lighthouse, but of course that wasn't an option anymore. Even outside in the yard felt different. Though nobody said it, Eli knew they were all self-conscious that the nosy girls next door would be watching, maybe thinking their games were stupid. At least Janie had left, which felt to Eli like a definite improvement. But even so, it was strange having kids so close by. He had tried to explain it all to his friend Anna, who lived on a farm in Maine. But he wasn't sure even she would understand. He wasn't used to having Rock Island feel weird. So now here he was, crammed in the van while Dad and Sam fought over the radio. Finally they pulled into the tiny parking lot.

Eli untangled himself and clambered out. Town was busy, as everyone took advantage of the rare cloudy day to run errands. The general store was mobbed and there was a line forming next to the one fancy-ish restaurant on the island, the Sisterhood. Sam was staring at it longingly. . . . It had the best clam chowder ever.

Eli walked toward the corner, where the road turned down to the water. From there he could smell the brine of the fish being cleaned at the dock.

"Let's walk down to the docks and see if Captain Jim is there," he said. "We need to get some answers about the lighthouse." The boys had discussed and pulled apart the information Val had shared, but they hadn't found out anything more, let alone anything important, like when the lighthouse might be open again.

Jax nodded. "Come on, Sam. There's no way we're going to the Sisterhood today. Way too crowded."

Sam gave a last longing look, then followed his brothers toward the dock.

"Stay together, please," Dad said, grabbing Frog's hand. "We'll meet you down there."

"I'll get good stuff!" Frog said importantly. "Maybe we can get blueberry muffins!"

"Nice try, Froggie," Dad said, pulling him toward the store. "Papa calls those second-mortgage muffins for a reason. . . . It would cost a hundred dollars to feed us all. How about you get to choose the cookies?"

Frog yelped in excitement and they disappeared into the building, leaving the three older boys on the sidewalk.

"Why does everything good have to cost money?" Jax asked as they walked.

Eli considered this. The island was really expensive, he knew. But that was because everything had to come over on the ferry, other than the stuff they bought from the one big farm, like corn, tomatoes, and other vegetables. And fish. They could buy fish from Captain Jim or one of the other fishermen on the docks, and that was pretty cool. But blueberry muffins were not something that could grow locally, he guessed.

"We could try to make muffins," he said. "Then they wouldn't cost as much."

"Or we could sell them! And we'd make all that money!" Jax said. He tripped on the warped and splintery wooden dock and nearly went flying into a bin of fish.

"Whoops! Careful there, sailor!" Captain Jim grabbed Jax by the elbow before he hit the fish. "Welcome back! I was hoping I would see you around here."

Captain Jim Fish—yes, his last name was really Fish, and he was a fisherman—had been born on the island, as had his parents. He had known Papa since forever, and always had a new story or treat for the boys when they saw him. Today was no different. Captain Jim reached around to his "office," which was a big wooden table with a locking drawer on the side of the dock, and grabbed a telltale brown bag with a red ribbon on the handle.

"Thought I might see you soon, so I swung over to Aunt Sarah's Sweets and picked this up. Well, picked up the first bag a few days ago, but I ate it all. Can't be surprised by that, can you now? Anyway, I went back and got more and locked it in the drawer so's to keep my hands to myself." He grinned and handed around the bag of Aunt Sarah's famous fudge.

With a loud overlapping babble of heartfelt thank-yous, everyone reached in and grabbed a chunk of dark chocolaty deliciousness. Sam hummed a little with happiness as he chewed.

"Hits the spot, doesn't it? I swear there's witchcraft involved in this fudge. It shouldn't be so darn good." Captain Jim put the bag away and turned back to the boys. "Now. How are you boys doing? Having a good summer, I hope? What do you think about your new neighbors? They have a couple of kids your age. . . . That has to be fun, right?"

Eli nodded politely. "It's pretty good. But, Captain Jim, can you tell us what's going on with the lighthouse?"

Sam, who had been staring at the bag of fudge, swung around. "Yeah, what's up? It's for sale? And then someone got hurt? What's the story?"

Captain Jim shook his head. "Well, that's part of the story. But not the bad part." He paused and looked around. "This is sort of confidential, meaning I'm supposed to keep my trap zipped."

"Please! Please, Captain Jim!" Jax said.

"Seriously, we're freaking out!" Sam added.

Eli didn't say anything but just looked at Captain Jim.

Captain Jim sighed. "Well, I shouldn't have said anything at all, I suppose. I'm getting as bad as the librarians . . . they're the biggest gossips on the island. But I figure you kids are practically islanders, and heck, it's going to be in the paper soon enough." He sighed, and Eli's heart sank. Whatever it was didn't sound good.

"What happened was this. The lighthouse was in kind of a bad way, from a fix-up point of view. The paint was peeling, and that led to the plaster under the paint crumbling, and *that* led to it looking a bit like the dog's dinner, from the outside, at least. And it turns out the light itself will need some mighty pricey upgrades within the next ten years. Now, lighthouses are the federal government's problem, and they have a heap of other problems, most of which are far more important. So all around New England, the Feds have been selling off lighthouses to private buyers. The buyers have to keep them running, and have to let the Coast Guard do their thing, but beyond that . . . the sky's the limit. The new owners can turn them into hotels, or private homes, or they can keep them open to the public. Anyway, we had hopes that a group of islanders could raise the money to buy the lighthouse, but once these repairs came up . . . well, our pockets are just about turned inside out, and an off-islander made an offer to buy it. Then, unfortunately, he got conked on the head with some falling stone, which I guess loosened when the plaster crumbled. He was okay, but he got scared pretty good." Captain Jim sighed and looked around again.

"And here's the latest news, and it's not pretty. This artist fellow's so concerned about public safety that he's convinced the town to keep the lighthouse closed until some surveyors can find out just how much damage there is." He looked away from the boys. "The worry is, if the damage is too bad, they'll have to tear it down and build another one, modern-like, to do the job."

"Tear it down!" Jax, Sam, and Eli all spoke at once.

"How is that fair?"

"Why would they do that?"

"Who is this guy?"

Captain Jim held up his hands. "Easy, tigers! I don't have all the answers. Just telling you what I heard. There's got to be an inspection, and the folks around here will raise what money we can. They'll kick up quite a fuss before anyone takes a wrecking ball to it. But meanwhile it's off-limits."

"But really, how can that even be an option? It's a historic . . . whatever, isn't it?" Eli asked. He was so flustered he was forgetting his words. The lighthouse was famous! It was mentioned in some major old whaling book, and a movie had even been filmed there. How could it just be torn down?

Captain Jim nodded. "It's on the National Register, but that doesn't grease the skids, as my dad used to say." He saw their questioning faces, and added, "That means it doesn't pay anything. The government's going to take the cheap road, and you can't blame them. There's a lot of fixing up needed around the country. Can't make every lighthouse the most important one."

The fisherman looked at them, and Eli imagined they looked pretty bad, because he slapped a hand down on the fish-gutting counter with a bang. "Now! Enough of the bad news. What else can I tell you? Ah, I know! Did I tell you about the new baby seals on Tuckernocket? Cutest little buggers I've seen in my life, and I've been around a bit. If your folks say it's okay I'll take you out on the boat to see 'em. Or is this the year you're going to paddle yourselves out there? I've heard some such talk, right?"

"We *would* be kayaking out there this year. If Eli wasn't such a wimp," Jax said, glaring at his brother.

"No need to be scared," Captain Jim said. "Choose a nice calm day and let me know, and I'll have the Coast Guard keep a beady eye on you. You'll be safe as kittens!"

Eli pressed his lips together. He knew Captain Jim was trying to be nice, but his stomach lurched from one miserable thought to the next. The lighthouse was in danger! And it would take a ton of money to fix it. And now the stupid kayaking again! Since when was it a crime not to want to be in a tiny tippy boat in the open ocean? He was an okay swimmer, but nothing special. And every time he sat in one of those boats it wobbled and slid like it wanted to throw him out.

"We should probably get back to Dad and Frog," he said, trying to ignore the lump in his stomach. The day had soured badly, and he just wanted to get home.

Captain Jim looked at him, and Eli tried not to look

away. The captain's face was thoughtful, and he held Eli's gaze.

"An awful lot of old dogs who work on this dock were pretty scared of the water when they first got here," he said finally. "And they're the smart ones. It's a good thing to be a little careful round the water, especially off Rock Island, when the tides and currents can give you a ride you weren't expecting. But your folks are pretty savvy. If they're with you I don't think you'll have anything to worry about."

Eli nodded, but he didn't say what he was thinking, which was that even with Dad and Papa he didn't trust that stupid boat to stay where he wanted it to.

Captain Jim just laughed a little. "You're smart *and* stubborn! A dangerous combination, on land or sea! I tell you what, if you kayak out to Tuckernocket, I'll let you name the new seal pup we have at the marine center. Poor little thing was abandoned by her mama over on Surf Beach. Probably got spooked by some fool tourists taking photos. No offense to the present company, but some people don't know how to leave wild things alone. Anyway, she's a sweet little thing, and, Eli, if you make the trip, we'll see if you can't get naming rights."

At this Eli's head came up. The marine center rescued any and all wild animals, and the Fletchers loved to visit. Imagine a tiny seal pup, named by him! But the kayak . . . He sighed and shrugged.

Captain Jim laughed. "Well, you can ponder it and let me know. And tell that Frog boy of yours to come see me. We've got some fun new friends at the marine center."

The boys nodded and headed back up the dock. All thoughts of blueberry muffins were gone, from Eli's mind at least. His brain was a swirling mess of worry over the lighthouse and unhappiness over kayaking. He couldn't seem to stop the two bad thoughts from fighting for his attention, each making him feel worse than the other. By the time they made it back to the van he was ready to cry.

Dad was loading groceries as they arrived.

"You weren't supposed to come back yet! I wanted to walk down to see Captain Jim," Frog wailed from the backseat.

Eli ignored him and climbed in.

"The lighthouse might be torn down!" Jax blurted out. "Captain Jim told us!"

"*What?*" Dad dropped a grocery bag into the back. "Darn it. I hope that wasn't the eggs," he muttered. "Anyway, what's this all about?"

Sam spoke from the front seat. "It's true. Captain Jim wasn't supposed to tell us, but it's going to be in the paper anyway. The federal government owns the lighthouse and they're selling it. Captain Jim says that a lot of lighthouses get sold but stay open to the public. And people here were raising money to buy it, but this artist guy wanted to buy it. Then he got hurt and apparently the lighthouse needs more repairs than anyone thought. So the artist dude still plans to buy it, but before he does he's having some inspectors come from off-island to make sure it's okay. And if it's not okay . . ." He paused. "If it's not okay," he repeated, "the government will probably tear it down and build some modern one."

There was silence in the van as Dad finished loading the groceries and slammed the back door. He seemed at a loss for words. Outside the gray clouds had finally given in and it started to rain. Eli stared at the drops on the window.

"Well," Dad said finally, as he backed out of the parking lot and started along the winding road home. "Let's wait and see what happens. The lighthouse has been here a long time, and survived a lot. I bet it can survive this too."

But Eli could tell from Dad's voice that he wasn't sure. Leaning his face against his arm, he let a few hot tears fall before swallowing the rest. He took a deep breath. It wasn't over yet. Maybe.

All that night Eli tossed and turned, eventually sitting up to stare past Jax's sleeping form and out the window, to the lighthouse. At least the light still worked, turning on automatically at dusk every day and sweeping its giant beam through the sleeping loft in a steady, reassuring pattern, like it had every year before.

Eli was wide-awake. Without his glasses everything

was blurry, but in the on-again, off-again flash of the lighthouse he could see his brothers sleeping around him, and farther out the window, the sweep and hollows of the moors. His mind darted to the idea of the lighthouse being gone, then just as quickly darted away. It could be saved. It *would* be saved! He took a deep breath, trying not to let the panicky feelings overtake him. His mind wandered . . . to Captain Jim telling him about the baby seal, to the scary thought of kayaking out to the island, to the blueberry muffins that Dad had broken down and bought for breakfast in the morning, even though they cost a lot of money. Money . . . man, if they had known about the lighthouse, they could have donated the money to save it instead! Eli's thoughts paused on that; then he darted out of bed and shook Jax awake.

"Huh? Wazzgoinon? Wazzamatter?" Jax said, bolting upright. He stared around in confusion.

"Shhh!" Eli whispered, but he felt like shouting, he was so excited. "It's just me. I had an idea. A really good one! What if we can raise enough money to save the lighthouse? Like those fund-raisers for donations . . . why can't we do one of those? I bet if we tried we could save it!"

Chapter Seven

IN WHICH THE FLETCHERS RISE TO THE OCCASION, BUT THEN SOME OF THEM SINK AGAIN

CAPTAIN JIM'S ISLAND NEWS
August 9, 8:15 a.m.

Well, the fair winds and following seas we're having these days are causing some folks to get a little giddy! If the person who hung the Montreal Canadiens flag up the town hall flagpole could come retrieve it before the Boston Bruins fans light it on fire, that would be great. It's not hockey season yet, folks. Meanwhile, go Red Sox!

Sam personally believed that vacations were all about sleep, and his right to have as much of it as possible. Of course, a sleeping loft with his three brothers and a window with no curtain meant that he had to work hard to sleep late, but Sam was nothing if not committed. He burrowed his head under his pillow and tried to block out all the noise and light.

"Sam! Get up, already! It's practically nine o'clock!" Jax was pulling at his blankets, but Sam held firm. He had learned how to hold on to his bedding while still remaining mostly asleep.

"Fine. I'll just eat the last blueberry muffin. The one Dad said we couldn't touch because it was yours. Then Eli and I will finish making our plans for the lighthouse fund-raiser without you!"

Sam opened his eyes. "Stay away from my muffin, if you don't want to suffer head injuries," he growled.

Jax just shrugged. "Um . . . okay, tough guy. Sure I will. Dad says that if you're not—"

But Sam had had enough. With a bound he was out of bed and running across the loft toward Jax, who gave a preemptive shriek before Sam even touched him.

"I WAS KIDDING! Your muffin is right there! Don't kill me!" Jax bellowed, moving as fast as he could down the ladder.

Sam glared down at him. Jax stared back up, then started to laugh. "You have to admit, 'stay away from my muffin' is a pretty hilarious thing to say," he said, lowering his voice to imitate Sam's growl.

Sam couldn't help laughing too. "It would be a good band name," he said, swinging down the ladder. "And fine, you win. I'm up. Now, with the question of my muffin's safety put to rest, what else were you babbling about?"

Eli and Frog circled closer as soon as Sam's feet hit the

floor, reminding him of a bunch of seagulls at the beach. Especially after Frog spilled pretzels. He waved them away. "Back off. I need to eat before anything else."

"We can talk *while* you eat," Eli said, handing him a plate with a massive, gorgeous, and mercifully unsullied blueberry muffin on it. "Come on!"

Sam let his brothers lead him out to the back deck, where a perfect summer day was waiting. The air was bright and crisp and dry, the last of the rain blown out to sea by the fast-moving breeze that shook the tall grass and trees. Sam collapsed in a deck chair with a sigh of happiness.

"Now, this," he said, taking a massive bite of the muffin, "is more like it."

It took the boys all of breakfast—which for Sam consisted of the muffin, two bowls of granola, a frozen bagel, and two containers of yogurt ("They're tiny!" he protested, when Papa rolled his eyes)—for his brothers to explain their idea.

"Think about it," Eli said finally. "Remember when we helped raise money for the town skating rink in Shipton? The town said they had no funds but would donate the land, and all in all I think they raised . . . oh, like thousands of dollars!"

"Three hundred thousand," Sam said indistinctly,

around a bite of yogurt. "We had a bunch of word problems about it in math last year."

"Three hundred thousand dollars!" Eli was silent for a second. "Well, if Shipton can raise all that for a brand-new ice rink, I bet Rock Island can raise enough for some repairs."

"Hey, check this out," Jax said. He held up the *Rock Island Inquirer,* the weekly newspaper, which Dad had left on the table.

The boys gathered around. The headline read ISLAND LIGHTHOUSE REPAIRS TO BE ASSESSED, and the article talked about an outside construction firm coming in to give an estimate on the work. The article included a quote from the artist, Chase Kark, who had gotten hurt at the lighthouse but still wanted to buy it. Kark said, "It pains me to imagine this beautiful place without the historic and original lighthouse. But public safety must come before art, and while I'm grateful my injuries were minor, I'm deeply afraid of what could happen next time."

Chewing thoughtfully, Sam looked at the photo of Chase Kark. He supposed it must have been pretty scary to have rocks crashing down all around, but he couldn't help thinking the guy looked like a loser. He scowled at the photo, then turned away.

"Okay. So some off-island guys are figuring out what it costs, and you want to have a bunch of lemonade stands and other stuff to raise money to help the town buy it and fix it up? Is that the basic idea?" Sam was beginning to feel tired again as the food hit his system. He lay down on the lounge chair and gazed up at the sky, where tiny, puffy white clouds were scudding past in the breeze.

"Yep. I have a list," Eli said, and thrust a yellow notepad at Sam.

Sam scanned the list. *Lemonade stand at the dock. Lobster races near the dock, with lobsters "borrowed" from one of Captain Jim's friends. Talent show. Yard sale.*

Sam looked up. "How are we going to have a yard sale? There's no one here but us and the Galindos. And what are we going to sell?"

"I thought we'd bring stuff into town. And we could sell old board games—"

"We could sell the old Scrabble," Jax said. "It's missing both *U*s, and Eli brought the one from home this year. Also I could sell my collar shirts. I hate them."

"I don't know who's going to buy a Scrabble game with no *U*," Sam said, "and anyway, I'm not sure Dad and Papa are going to be too jazzed about us selling off our clothes. But I guess I'm in for the other stuff. But later, like this afternoon. It's awesome out. Let's go to the beach!"

It was a flawless beach day. The storm had blown away, leaving only massive curling waves and the odd piece of driftwood washed up on the shore. For hours, Sam flung himself on his boogie board and let the waves pull and smash him into the sand, stopping only long enough to wolf down three pieces of cold barbecue chicken and a couple of peaches. The air smelled of salt and sticky peach juice and the sunscreen that Dad kept reminding them to put on. Overhead, gulls squawked and called, wheeling white against the blue of the sky.

Nearby Jax and Eli were shrieking, playing their favorite game of Tackle the Waves, which mostly involved flinging themselves into the roiling surf over and over. Finally, they all lay exhausted on their towels. Sam's eyes were stinging from the salt and his skin was pleasantly cold to the touch. Next to him, his brothers buzzed with ideas for the lemonade stand, which they had determined was the easiest place to start.

"We need a big Save the Lighthouse banner," Eli said. He had sat up and was absently burying Frog in the hot sand as they planned. "Maybe we can use an old sheet or something. It has to be big. Big enough that everyone can see it."

"Where are we going to hang it?" Jax asked.

Sam, who finally felt awake after a fourth piece of chicken and one more quick dunk in the ocean, sat up. "We can hang it on the side of one of the boats, maybe? Captain Jim would probably let us, if he's around. Or we can always tack it up on the dock pilings."

Papa, who had decided to play hooky from work for

the morning, looked over at Dad, who nodded his head a little. Papa cleared his throat loudly.

"What?" Eli said, pausing mid-scoop. "Why are you making that 'ahem' sound?"

Papa looked at Dad again, then sighed. "Look, boys, we think it's a great idea to hold fund-raisers for the lighthouse. It will let people know how important this is, and it's a wonderful gesture. But . . ."

He trailed off. Sam looked down at his towel. He knew where Papa was going with this.

"It's unlikely that you guys will be able to raise the full amount needed to do the repairs. It's going to take a lot of money, more than is reasonable to expect to make in a few weeks," Dad said, when it became clear Papa wasn't going to continue.

Eli kept digging. "Of course we know that!" he said. "But you never know. Maybe others will join in, and we'll get a ton of people involved. It worked for the ice rink in Shipton!"

Dad and Papa both nodded. "It's true. You never know," Papa said, smiling. "You just never know, in this world."

Sam sat up and grabbed another sandwich. "Okay!" he said, shoving half of it into his mouth and swallowing in two big gulps. "Back to work!"

Finally the plan was set, and Dad agreed to bring them into town for the all-important late-afternoon tourist-shopping hours.

Back at the house, they concocted a lemonade from frozen concentrate and fresh-squeezed lemons, complete with slices of lemon and fresh mint from the pot on the patio.

"Looks fancy!" Frog said, sounding impressed.

"Tastes delicious!" Sam answered, downing a cup.

Eli shot him a look. "No more! We need to sell it!"

"I'm quality control," Sam protested, but he rinsed out the cup and went to get his flip-flops.

When they got to the docks, Eli took charge.

"Okay, set the table up here," he directed Sam, who was hauling a folding table. "And, Jax, see if you can tack the banner up behind me, on the pilings."

Within a few minutes Sam had to admit it looked pretty cool. The banner had been overseen by Jax, whose artistic representation of the lighthouse was pretty spot-on. It was tacked to the tall wooden pilings that lined the dock. The giant letters could be seen practically from the street, and the red-striped lighthouse was unmistakable.

As they were admiring it, they heard a familiar voice.

"Oooh, *muy impresionante*!" Val said, staring. "Very artistic!" She nodded approvingly. "I'll get a shot of you all standing by the sign. I'll use it in my summer memories film. Move closer, you guys."

Jax glanced at Sam, then scooted closer, pulling Eli along. Frog jumped in front.

"Did you come into town to get our lemonade?" Frog asked, as Val moved slowly side to side, presumably getting whatever arty shot she was after. "Your hat is *so* pretty!"

"Oh, I was at the island's improv group," Val said, turning off the phone. "I film them when I have time. You should see them . . . they're hilarious." She grinned, turning to leave. "Good luck, *chicos*!" she called over her shoulder. "Hope you get lots of money!"

They watched her walk away, her enormous rainbow-striped sun hat trying to escape in the breeze.

"I like her," Frog said. "She always has exciting outfits."

Sam shrugged. "She's okay. A lot better without her weird friend, that's for sure." It was true. While at first Janie and Val had seemed to be two of a kind, both girlie girls who giggled and said stupid things, today, with Janie gone, he had to admit that Val seemed normal. Other than her wild outfits, of course.

Eli waved his hands impatiently. "Now remember," he said, "we aren't charging for the lemonade. We're *accepting donations*."

"But how will we make any money?" Frog looked worried. "We can't just give it away!"

"Don't worry, buddy," Sam said. "Eli's right. People give way more than we would charge. Wait and see."

As though in response, an older woman with three young children came over to the table. Eli immediately straightened up.

"Would you like some lemonade?" he asked politely.

"All donations are going to help fix the Rock Island lighthouse!"

"I read about that in the paper," the woman said, pulling out her wallet. "Well, that's a good cause, don't you think?"

Her kids nodded in unison, and Eli started to hand out cups.

"It's homemade!" Frog piped up. "Well, mostly homemade, with some mix too, because we got a little tired squeezing lemons."

Jax kicked him under the table and Sam rolled his eyes, but the woman just laughed. "That seems entirely reasonable. Too much squeezing will sour a person, I think. Here you go, and good luck!"

The boys watched in amazement as she dropped a twenty-dollar bill into their clearly marked DONATIONS jar.

"Um . . . thank you! Wow! Thank you so much! That's really generous. THANK YOU!" Eli babbled, until Sam kicked *him* under the table.

When the woman walked away, the boys high-fived each other.

"This is going to be easy!" Jax yelled.

"I told you. Donations are the way to go," Eli said smugly.

Sam took advantage of the celebration to gulp a quick cup of lemonade. It really was good.

A steady stream of other visitors, not quite as outrageous but still generous, kept them busy. The afternoon had gotten warmer and warmer as the breeze died, and the air was still and hot.

"Ew, a bug fell in," Frog said, peering into the giant glass dispenser that held the lemonade. He fished it out with his finger but managed to spill a cup of lemonade in the process. The sweet, sticky liquid splashed all over Sam.

"Ugh! Frog! I'm covered in . . . Hey, is that a bee?" Sam asked. He hated bees. Like, really hated them. He tensed, looking around.

Sure enough, the sweet drink had attracted more than just generous donations. To Sam's horror, his lemonade-scented legs and T-shirt were drawing the buzzing bugs right toward him.

"Get them away! Get off! GO!" Sam yelled, bobbing and weaving and waving his arms. An angry buzz swooped right by his ear. "ARGH! Go! AWAY!" he shouted again.

"Stop it! You're just making them mad! Chill out!" Eli yelled, but it was too late.

Two angry buzzing sounds were now circling Sam's head while others zoomed ominously close to his legs. Sam ran from the table, or tried to, but his foot got caught in the strap of the bag that held their money and the extra cups. Flailing, he tried to regain his balance, and knocked over the glass lemonade jug.

"SAM!" Frog yelled, as a wave of lemonade poured over the table. "Ouch! OWWW! It stung me!"

Sam freaked. He lunged backward, forgetting the strap, forgetting his brothers, forgetting, somehow, that he was on a dock. He fell against the banner, which promptly pulled free from the pilings and dropped into the water. Sam, pinwheeling wildly, fell after it.

For a terrifying second he was wrapped up in the sheet, struggling to get free and back to the surface. But then he was out, his head popping up, gasping for breath.

"THE BAG! GET THE BAG!" his brothers screamed from the dock.

Sam treaded water and tried to blink the salt from his eyes. In front of him, sinking slowly and—oh no!—leaking dollar bills that floated briefly before dropping out of sight, was the tote bag. Desperately, Sam dived again and again, trying to grab as much of the money as possible before it sank. A crowd of people had gathered on the dock, including Captain Jim, who lowered a ladder and bellowed at Sam to get out of the water and stop being a fool. But Sam ignored him. Only when every single bill was flung up into the waiting hands of his brothers did Sam clamber out, dripping, exhausted, and deeply embarrassed.

Before him was a scene of carnage. Captain Jim's first mate had mostly finished picking up the broken glass, while another fisherman rinsed down the sticky bee-magnet dock. But still. The table was tipped over, and the banner, its paint ruined beyond recognition, was wadded up in a dripping pile. His brothers, all in varying degrees of dampness and tears, were staring at him.

Sam swallowed hard and accepted the towel Captain Jim held out. Then, silently, he gathered his brothers and started the long walk back toward the van.

Frog, his voice tiny and barely recognizable, reached for his hand and whispered, "Sam, what *happened*?"

Sam could only answer, "I really hate bees."

The drive home was silent.

Chapter Eight

IN WHICH ELI FINDS IT HARD TO BALANCE

Boys, strange to say, but I found some good old-fashioned cash money tangled around my lines when I hauled them up this morning. There was even a twenty-dollar bill! Since the fish round these parts tend to use the barter system rather than U.S. legal tender, I figured the money might just belong to you.

Best, Captain Jim

P.S. If you leave bees alone, they generally leave you alone. Just a tip.

Eli was mad at Sam, even though he felt bad about the whole scared-of-bees thing. After all, Sam wasn't really scared of much. Well, except for most bugs. But the fact was, his freak-out had really dampened the enthusiasm for the fund-raising, both literally and figuratively. They'd salvaged most of the money, though of course any coins had been lost to the harbor bottom. And Jax had painted a new banner. But neither his brothers nor his parents seemed ready for the next project, which was supposed to be the lobster races. In fact, even Captain Jim had strongly suggested they take a day off and let the dust—or lemonade—settle, before returning to the docks. Worse, he then offered to bring over his extra kayak so that all the Fletchers could head down to the cove.

So not only was Eli *not* working toward getting back into the lighthouse, he was standing on the rocky cove shore, staring with extreme mistrust at the skinny boat in front of him.

"Now, it's as calm as a lake today, and we're going to stay close to shore, okay, buddy? And you're wearing your PFD, and it's a good one. So . . ."

Dad let his voice trail off. Eli knew the facts. He understood that Calm Seas + Shoreline + Personal Flotation Device = Perfectly Safe. The equation worked. The only problem was that he didn't really believe it.

Still, Eli nodded. Bravely, he hoped. "Sure. I got it," he said, trying to sound confident. "Where's everyone else?"

"I thought we'd take a paddle together first, just the two of us," Dad said. "They're climbing over the far rocks with Papa."

Eli closed his eyes for a second. He would rather be

climbing the rocks, maybe finding sea urchins or even seeing seals. But no. His fate was to wobble in a tiny boat.

With Dad's help he pushed the kayak into the water and positioned himself in the tiny seat.

"Ready for the paddle?" Dad asked.

"Ready," Eli said, taking the double paddle in both hands, dipping one end into the water and pushing off.

The boat swung wildly, and Eli couldn't help giving a tiny shriek. "I'm fine! I'm fine. Just . . . surprised myself," he said, through clenched teeth.

Dad quickly jumped into his own kayak and pushed off, paddling cleanly and excellently to catch up with Eli, who was drifting with the current.

"You look great, buddy! Like a real pro!" Dad called.

Eli smiled. Or at least he tried to smile, though it felt more like a grimace.

"Let's head along the shore, just practicing, okay?" Dad said, dipping one end of his paddle, then the other, into the water.

Eli followed suit, barely daring to look up from the water as he pushed the paddle up and down, up and down. Slowly, his breathing calmed. Dad was right. The water was totally flat, and if Eli was really careful the boat barely wobbled. He even glanced up from time to time, taking in the line of the horizon, the sky a perfect flat blue against the dark green of the water. In the distance a motorboat buzzed and hummed, but nearby all he heard was the slap of the water against the kayak and the occasional cry of the seagulls.

"Look how far we've come," Dad said, turning in his boat and gesturing back at the beach.

Eli turned to look, but the boat swung, so he quickly faced forward again. It was going pretty well, he had to admit. He could almost understand why his brothers liked this so much. It was cool, sliding through the water, seeing the familiar Rock Island landscape from sea instead of land. Far out, a cormorant was perched on a lobster buoy, its wings outstretched in the breeze. Eli smiled at Dad.

"That's what I like to see!" Dad said, smiling back. "Check out how close we are to the far rocks. Keep an eye out—we might see your brothers. Won't they be surprised to see us all the way over here!"

Eli and Dad paddled along, looking for the family, their paddles dipping into the water almost in tandem.

"Did you know that Captain Jim said I might be able to name the orphaned seal pup at the marine lab? Just me, not the others."

Dad nodded. "He told me. He even said he'd let us do some field research on Tuckernocket if we go out there. Pretty cool. Now, what are you thinking about for names?"

"Well, I've got a couple of options. I thought about Anna, because she named one of the farm's baby goats after me, so I thought she'd be psyched to have a seal named after her. But then I thought about Cassiopeia, since I've always loved that constellation, and because she could be Cassie for short. Or—"

Before Eli could offer the next name, there was a tremendous lurch and the kayak swung wildly from side to side.

"DADDY!" he screamed, trying to keep from tipping over.

"It's okay! Just pull your paddle up! Hang in there!" Dad called, trying to paddle through the suddenly wild and churning water.

"I'm going to tip! What's happening?" Eli screamed. The boat was rocking as the huge waves buffeted it, slapping hard against its side and nearly tipping it over.

"Hang on! It's that . . ." Dad trailed off into a stream of swears that surprised Eli, even in the midst of his fear. Dad *never* swore.

"—speedboat! It was going *way* too close to shore! We just got hit by its wake. See, it's already almost gone," Dad said, trying to sound calm, and failing. His sunglasses had fallen off and his face was red and mad.

"Whoever was driving that thing was going *WAY* too fast, and *WAY* too close to shore. That should have never happened. Are you okay?" Dad asked.

Eli shook his head speechlessly. His hands clutched the paddle and he had to blink back tears.

"That was scary, buddy. I know. But hey! You're okay, right? You didn't even tip. And if you had, your life jacket would have kept you safe, right?" Dad's voice was calmer now, but Eli didn't care.

All the good thoughts about kayaking had fled. He swallowed hard, then said, "Can we go back now? Please?"

Dad sighed, and with a last nasty look at the receding speedboat, started to lead Eli back along the shore to the beach.

When they got there, the rest of the Fletchers were waiting. Even from a distance Eli could hear a scary sort of yowling.

"You're back! I was going to see if Zeus likes the ocean more than the bathtub!" Frog shouted, jumping up and down on the sand.

Eli jumped out of the kayak, pulled it far enough up on the beach that it wouldn't float away, and stalked off, not bothering to answer his brother.

"What's wrong? Don't you want to see Zeusy swim?" Frog called after him.

But Eli didn't care. He went up to his towel and flung himself down. Behind him Dad was explaining.

"He did great, really. He was like a pro. But then some"—Dad paused, probably to swallow the terrible swearwords he'd said before—"moron in a speedboat swung way too close and we got hit by the wake. It was a little scary."

Eli closed his eyes, enjoying the solid ground underneath him.

Later, after Frog learned that Zeus emphatically did NOT like swimming in the ocean any better than the bathtub, and Zeus had nearly taken off Jax's leg attempting to get away from the water, Frog and Papa brought Zeus back to the house. The rest of the family sprawled out, consuming a massive picnic along the rocky shore. Eli had joined them to eat, though he didn't share in his brothers' conversation about who would go out in the kayaks next, or how fun it would be to race to the far rocks. He just moodily munched his sandwich, barely bothering to reach across Jax's barrier of towels and sand buckets for the potato chips.

He was trying to think of an excuse to go home when the speedboat roared back into the cove, this time coming closer and closer to shore before cutting its engine and stopping. In the sudden silence the boys could clearly hear the boat's radio blasting about Zaztax stock going through the roof. A man stood at the stern and threw an anchor overboard. Then he jumped over the side of the boat into the shallow water and waded ashore, holding a giant wooden box above his head to keep it dry.

"Ahoy there!" he called as he waded in. "Looks like a lovely day for a picnic."

Dad stood. Eli straightened up to see what would happen next. Dad was usually really polite, and very slow to anger. Papa was the one who got mad. But Dad looked seriously cheesed.

"You!" Dad said, and his tone added *moron*. "Do you realize how fast you were going before? Our kayaks were nearly knocked over by your wake, and my son was quite frightened. While there are no speed limits that I know of in the cove, courtesy, as well as basic common sense, should tell you not to speed through here like a maniac!"

The man brought his hands to his face. Eli thought he looked like he was miming the word *remorse* in charades.

"Oh no! I'm terribly sorry. I was so focused on scouting for a new painting spot that I wasn't paying attention. But that's no excuse, of course. Really. I apologize. To all of you." The man looked around at the boys, as though wondering which one he had traumatized. His eyes lingered a little on Jax, then flicked away.

Eli looked down.

Dad nodded a little, his face smoothing out a bit. "Apology accepted. But please be careful in the future. Rock Island isn't really a place for speed."

The man nodded enthusiastically. "So true! It's a place to slow down and enjoy the beauty of it! I couldn't agree more. Again, I'm just so sorry. I wish I could make it up to you, but I can promise I'll never do it again. Sincerely." He put one hand over his heart.

Eli thought, again, of a game of charades.

He continued. "May I introduce myself? I'm Chase Kark." He held out his hand to Dad.

Chase Kark was wearing a faded pinkish-red button-down shirt, a pair of bright green shorts, and a visor. His blond hair was barely ruffled, despite the speedboat ride.

Dad shook his hand, smiling slightly, but he still looked a little put out. "Tom Anderson. This is Sam, Jax, and Eli," he said, pointing to each of them in turn. "My youngest son and my husband, Jason Fletcher, will be back shortly."

"The Fletchers!" Chase Kark said, smiling at all of them with big, shiny white teeth. "I've heard your names before. You live next to the lighthouse!"

"And you're the artist who got hurt there! And now you want to buy it!" Eli blurted out. He had just remembered where he had heard Kark's name before.

Kark's smile dimmed, but just a bit. "That was me, sadly," he said, not sounding terribly sad. "But I'm fine, and hey—you know what they say: you have to suffer for art. Hopefully the painting came out well." He smiled again. "The lighthouse is a magnificent piece of the island's heritage. It would be an honor to own it. But safety *must* come first!"

"But will it be private? I mean, will people still be able to go in?" Sam asked.

Kark's smile, if possible, grew larger. "I would never

want to deprive people of the opportunity to access such a lovely spot," he said, his hand over his heart again.

"But does that mean—" Sam started, but then the familiar sound of the ice cream truck drifted over from the parking lot.

"ICE CREAM TRUUUUUUUUUUUUUUCK!" Frog screamed, appearing by the edge of the parking lot as well. He and Papa were back, without the yowling cat. "HEY, GUYS, LOOK! IT FOLLOWED US HERE!"

Chase Kark reached into his pocket. "It's the least I can do," he said, handing Sam a bill. "Ice cream's on me. If that's okay, of course," he added, glancing at Dad.

Dad looked annoyed, but nodded.

"Is this a fifty?" Sam asked, staring at the bill.

"Just bring me the change whenever I see you next. I trust you!" Chase Kark said, picking up the wooden box and walking toward the far rocks. "I'm off to set up my easel and take advantage of this great landscape. Lovely to meet you all." And with that, he was gone.

The boys looked at each other.

"A fifty," Sam said, his voice disbelieving.

"Let's go!" Jax yelled, running toward the truck.

Eli followed slowly. He felt bad, like there was a lump in his stomach, but he wasn't sure if it was just leftover queasiness from the kayak, or something bigger, something as big as a giant red-and-white-striped lighthouse. Trying to shake it off, he started to run. After all, ice cream was worth running for, even after a terrible day.

Chapter Nine

IN WHICH BRUNCH INCLUDES A SIDE ORDER OF SURPRISE

Jax, where are you guys?! Come over ASAP and bring the bug box! Found two green snakes and have them in my hat for now. Alex

Jax had to admit that in the few days they'd had on the island without Janie around, giggling and whispering, Valerie Galindo had improved *a lot*. She was obsessed with her video camera, it was true, forever trying to film them, which was a little annoying. And she wore the craziest clothes, even when they were just going to the beach. But with Janie gone there was no more talk about how cute Sam was, which was a relief, and it turned out she was pretty funny and a decent soccer player. Still, there was no question which Galindo kid was the real score. Alex was better at catching snakes than anyone

Jax had ever met. Jax loved to *watch* snakes, and didn't mind holding them, but he wasn't crazy about reaching into dark, damp places and trying to grab them. Alex was a pro.

Today, after relocating the two tiny green snakes Alex had found under the old tire from Alex's Chicago White Sox hat to the bug box, Jax and Alex were wrestling with Sir Puggleton and the Galindo-Greens' dog, Horatio. Horatio was a big Lab-husky mix who was only a year old, and Sir Puggleton had rediscovered his inner puppy when they played. Alex and Jax took turns flinging tennis balls and pulling them out of drooling dog mouths—neither dog was particularly good at giving the ball back—until they were exhausted. Then they lay back on the grass and clover of the yard, staring up at the sky.

They had just finished comparing their favorite foods, which had led to a discussion of their favorite places. Alex's list included at least four continents and foods Jax had never even heard of. But Alex's level of excitement upon hearing that the Fletchers' aunt Lucy was *the* Lucy of New York's Lucy's Cupcakes, made Jax feel better.

"Yeah, she's the coolest," he bragged, flopping onto his stomach. "She lets us test all the new flavors. She's coming later this summer. Her and her boyfriend, Elon. He's pretty awesome too. He's a magician . . . like, a really famous one." It was true. Elon worked at a well-known magic store near Lucy's apartment, but he also performed in theaters all around the country and sometimes around the world.

"A magician and a cupcake maker . . . man, your family is awesome." Alex sighed. "We barely have any family. Mami has a few ancient aunties and a kind of crazy uncle who lives in Texas and has a bunch of guns. We don't see him much. And Dad . . . well, he's actually our stepdad. That's why we have different last names. Anyway, his family was the one that had this house. But they're all dead. He calls himself an orphan and tries to get us to feel sorry for him."

"I'll share the cupcakes when Lucy and Elon come," Jax promised. "You'll just have to move fast to get them before Sam." He rolled onto his back and stared at the sky again. "Hey, Sam just told me this morning—did you know the Patriots picked up a new running back?"

Alex shrugged and rolled away. "Did I tell you I still don't care about the New England Patriots? Or any American football team? They're so lame! A bunch of fat guys in helmets. No thanks."

Jax waved his hand dismissively. This wasn't the first time they'd had this argument. Alex, who had grown up moving among London, Buenos Aires, and Chicago, adored soccer and the Chicago White Sox but didn't care about any other sports.

Before Jax could launch into yet another explanation about why real football was still awesome, even if it was slower than soccer, Val appeared. She was even more dressed up than usual, in some kind of bright patterned dress-and-scarf combination. Jax hoped she wasn't about to go ask Sam on a date or something.

But Val flopped down on the grass next to them. "Ay, it's so nice out here. I wish we didn't have to go to that stupid brunch. Daddy says at least we can go out on the boat after. He says we can bring food and stay out until sunset."

Alex groaned. "I forgot about brunch. It's so lame. I have no idea why we have to be at this thing. . . . It's honoring the island library or something. I've never even been *in* the library."

"Because Mami and Dad donated something, I'm sure," Val said with a sigh.

Jax didn't say anything. It was pretty clear—from the house, the boat, the places they'd traveled—that the Galindo-Green family had a lot of money. But mostly it didn't matter much. He knew their mom, Natalia, was some kind of semifamous businessperson, in places where businesspeople were famous. Jax hadn't even heard of Natalia's company, let alone her. But according to Alex, it could be a real pain when grown-ups sucked up to them to get to their mom. And their dad, who was one of the funniest people Jax had ever met, wrote travel books that were a really big deal, so he was pretty well known too. His family had owned the Wheelright house forever, though Jax had learned that the rest of his family had either moved far away or were dead.

"When do you have to go?" he asked, rolling over and looking in the grass for a four-leaf clover. So far he hadn't found one, but he was patient.

"Soon," Val answered. "Alex, you need to go get ready. Dad says you should wear a dress."

Jax laughed. Their dad really was hilarious. And he was always doing crazy things. He said it was because he was a writer. Alex groaned again and got up. "This is garbage. It's an awesome day and we're going to sit in a restaurant? Lame."

The Galindos went in, and Jax headed for home. When he got there, Papa was walking down the driveway.

"Oh good! You're home. I was just coming over to get you. We have the library benefit this morning. Take a quick—" He looked closely at Jax, who had grass in his hair and dirt on his hands and knees. "Take a *long* shower, then get dressed. No sport shorts, please, and wear a collared shirt."

"We're going to this thing too?" Jax asked, his voice rising in outrage. "What? We're not loaded! Why do *we* have to go?"

Papa gave him A LOOK. "Pardon me?"

Jax backpedaled. "Well, Val and Alex have to go because their parents gave money to the library. Why are we going?"

Papa gave him a gentle shove toward the house. "Well, let's see. Your grandmother has the local history room named after her, remember? And your great-grandmother helped start the original permanent library on the island. So yes, even though we are not 'loaded,' as you so nicely put it, we have a long history with the library. Now go shower!"

Jax shuffled off to the outdoor shower. "I'm going, I'm going," he said. "But I still think it's a waste of a perfect day."

The Appledore Inn was the only real hotel on the island, and one of its biggest buildings too. The Fletchers walked up the wide wooden steps and clomped across the giant shaded porch, where people sat in rocking chairs watching the boats bobbing in the harbor.

Jax snorted. What kind of people would come to Rock Island and sit on a porch, rather than actually going out and doing something? A few of them were pretty old, it was true, but Mimi and Boppa still went to the beach, even if they needed big upright chairs and an umbrella.

"I like this place," Frog said as they walked into the dim lobby. "I like the rocking chairs. And I like the pictures." He pointed at the walls, which were filled with enormous black-and-white photographs of Rock Island over the years.

"There's the lighthouse," Eli said, pointing at one.

"And there's Val and Alex's house," Jax added, looking at the photo.

"Where's our house?" Frog asked, peering at it.

Dad walked over. "See? It's this tiny shack right there." He pointed to a small blob on the photo. "This was before it was expanded, when it was just one room."

Jax stared. The Nugget looked like a doghouse next to the massive Wheelright house. But both houses were dwarfed by the lighthouse, standing tall and proud in the foreground of the photo. The boys stood for a second, looking at it. Jax figured they were all thinking the same thing.

Sam spoke first. "We'll get back to fund-raising tomorrow."

Papa gave him a quick hug. "Sounds good," he said, starting to walk toward the dining room. "But for now, let's get in there before we're late."

There was a crowd moving slowly through the doors into the dining room. As the Fletchers shifted and shuffled in line, a loud voice boomed out in front of them.

"What a worthy institution! I believe it was the poet T. S. Eliot who said that libraries were our best hope for the future. So glad to be able to join this event," the voice said.

Jax peered through the crowd and saw the blond, tan head of Chase Kark. He was waving his arms while he spoke, causing people around him to bob and weave slightly in order to avoid being whacked. As they filed into the room, Jax was relieved to see Kark going to a table near the front.

He was even more relieved, when they finally entered the fancy dining room, with its white tablecloths and vases of roses everywhere, to see that they were at a table with the Galindo-Green family, at least according to the seating chart.

Jax slid into his seat, glowering at Frog when he tried to sit next to him.

"Go sit somewhere else. I'm saving this for Alex."

Frog huffed, but moved over to sit by Eli. "I don't even want to sit with you. Eli said he'd help me with Zeus's swimming lessons. You won't even get a chance to help," he said.

Jax rolled his eyes. "If I am *never* near another soaking-wet cat in my life—*especially* a soaking-wet Zeus—that's soon enough for me! I still have scabs from his last 'swim.' " Jax pulled his leg up onto the chair to peer at his ankle, which was crisscrossed with scratches.

"Here come the Galindo-Greens," Papa said, waving an arm. "John! Over here."

Sam sighed a little as Val moved toward them, waving wildly, as though she hadn't seen them in days. Val was always theatrical.

Jax felt bad for him. Val was okay, but Alex was . . .

Alex was walking toward them, behind Natalia, wearing . . . a dress?

Jax stared, a grin blooming on his face. Was this a joke? How completely awesome! His parents would never let him get away with—

"Alexandra! You look very distinguished," Papa said, pretending to bow.

Alexandra? Jax paused, half in and half out of his chair. Alex wasn't wearing a baseball cap, which was weird. Jax took in the neatly combed ear-length hair, the big dark eyes that looked just like Val's, and the leather necklace with a whale's-tail pendant that Alex always wore. But now, with a fancy light blue T-shirt dress and sandals, it looked like an actual necklace. That a *girl* would wear.

Crash.

"Jax!" Dad cried. "Are you okay?"

Jax had tried to sit down and missed his chair completely, crashing to the ground.

"Huh? What? Oh. I'm, um . . . fine. I'm fine." Stumbling, Jax got up, barely noticing that his butt was throbbing where it had slammed into the hard wooden floor. He sat in the chair, careful to look anywhere but at Alex, who had taken the seat next to his.

"Why are you so weird? You turning into a freak show?" Alex *sounded* the same, at least.

But Jax couldn't bring himself to answer. All around him the grown-ups were jabbering and chatting, talking about the library and whether the low fish catch would turn around in the fall. Eli and Frog were staring at Alex, as though waiting for someone to explain what was going on. Jax knew how they felt.

"Hand me the butter, will you?" Alex asked, picking up a roll. "I'm starving."

Jax grabbed the silver dish in front of him and handed it over. He couldn't help noticing that Alex's hands, which had been holding snakes and crabs all week, looked suddenly small and clean and . . . dainty.

"What is *wrong* with you?" Alex asked loudly, and Jax jumped.

"Nothing!" he squawked, and jammed his knife into the butter, figuring it would be rock hard and cold. Instead it had softened to mush, and the pressure of Jax's hand turned his knife into a catapult, sending a wad of butter flying.

"Oh no!" Jax yelled. He watched in horror as the butter arced up into the air, then landed with an audible splat on the cheek of the woman at the table next to them.

"AAAAAAAH!" she shrieked, leaping up as though she'd been stung.

Jax stared, frozen.

Dad, who had started to rise out of his chair when the woman yelled, paused, staring from Jax's knife to the woman's face. He closed his eyes for a second.

"What happened?"

"Are you okay?"

"It's butter!"

"It's only butter!"

"Why is she covered in butter?"

"Where did it come from?"

Jax slid down in the chair, wishing he could slide under the table and disappear. Dad had rushed over to the other table, where the questions, exclamations, and apologies rang out loud and fast.

"Jackson! Why on earth . . ." Papa started; then he shook his head. "You know what? Never mind. There is absolutely nothing you can say that will make sense of the fact that you just flung butter . . ." He paused and put both hands over his face, scrubbing hard.

"I'm sorry!" Jax squeaked. "I just . . . It was an accident! I . . ."

Papa just waved his hand for silence, then covered his face again.

Jax slunk lower. How had the butter even *done* that? He didn't think he could do it again, even if he tried. He glanced out of the corner of his eye at the other table, where the woman was wiping her face with a large napkin while everyone at her table stood around her, talking loudly. Jax quickly stared at his lap.

Finally Papa looked up, red-faced, eyebrows rumpled. He took a deep breath.

"Okay. How about this?" He looked at all the boys in turn, ending with Jax. "New Fletcher Family rule. From now on, no flinging butter onto strangers. All right?"

"Or on family members or friends!" Dad added, sliding back into his chair. "Let's go ahead and make that a universal rule. No butter flinging at all!"

The boys nodded silently.

"No butter flinging at all," Frog whispered, sounding solemn.

Jax stared at the table. The butter had been so mushy! And Alex was in a dress! And— Well, it didn't matter. Papa was right. There was no point in trying to explain.

Glancing around, he caught Alex's eye. Alex had a napkin over his—her!—face.

"Are you . . . ," Jax started to ask. Now what? Was Alex crying? Who knows what a girl might do?

Alex dropped the napkin, and Jax saw that she was laughing so hard that tears were streaming down her face. Jax felt his own face relax; then he started to grin.

"You . . . ! That . . . ! Best. Thing. Ever!" Alex gasped between pants of laughter. "Her face . . ." She dissolved into laughter and couldn't finish.

Jax glanced over to the other table. Mercifully, everyone seemed to be smiling. His grin spread wider; then he started to laugh too.

"Next time . . . ," Alex tried to say, between gasps, ". . . and for the rest of my life . . . if someone says 'Pass the butter' "—she hiccupped—"I'm gonna picture . . ." Words escaped and the laughter took over.

Jax couldn't help it. He laughed harder; then Eli,

Frog, Sam, and Val were all laughing hysterically, miming Jax's butter flinging. Pretty soon Natalia, John, and even Dad and Papa were laughing so hard they could barely breathe.

Finally someone at the front of the room rang a bell, and all around them the guests fell quiet. Jax swallowed one last snort.

"Honored guests . . ." The woman at the front of the room began her speech, and Jax tried to settle down.

He glanced over at Alex. Now that he looked, really looked, at his friend, he supposed the whole girl thing was pretty obvious. But what was he supposed to think, with a name like Alex? And when she was always wearing board shorts and swim shirts on the beach, the same as Jax and his brothers? He sighed.

Alex looked over at him. "Butter?" she whispered, holding up the silver dish and grinning.

Chapter Ten

IN WHICH SAM SITS ON AN IMAGINARY BENCH TO PASS THE TIME

CAPTAIN JIM'S ISLAND NEWS
August 11, 6:00 a.m.

It's another glorious late-summer day on the island, and the sunshine is supposed to continue for the rest of the week. Meanwhile, everyone stay safe, in the water and out. And to the gentleman who was on the receiving end of the Heimlich maneuver at the Sisterhood last night, apologies. My wife honestly thought you were choking, and didn't realize you were just enjoying your chowder with gusto. Next meal is on us.

Sam wandered into the kitchen, then wandered back out again, empty-handed. Dad raised an eyebrow.

"You okay, buddy? What's going on?"

Sam shrugged. The day before, they'd gone back into town to try the lobster races, hoping to raise more money for the lighthouse. Of course, one of the lobsters had escaped over the dock. The boys had been forced to pay for it out of their donations, so it had been kind of an epic fail. Sure, they had saved most of the lemonade money, and even with the lost lobster they had made a little more yesterday, but the grand total wasn't exactly inspiring. They weren't going to buy a lighthouse with sixty-eight dollars. They couldn't even buy a brick. That morning they'd decided on a day off and headed to the big beach. It had been awesome, complete with perfect waves and some sick rides on his surfboard. But now they were home, in that dead time after the beach and before dinner, and Sam was . . . Sam was bored. On Rock Island. It was an unfamiliar and unpleasant feeling.

"Where are your brothers?" Papa asked from the porch, where he had been listening.

"Jax is over in Alex's yard, catching snakes, and Eli and Frog are with the stupid cat again," Sam answered.

As though in response there was a low yowling from the bathroom. Dad shuddered a little.

"That poor cat," he muttered. Then he stood up. "I'm going into town to get some fish for dinner. Want to come?"

Sam shrugged again, then nodded. His phone got a little service in town. Maybe he'd call Em, just to see how her rehearsals were going. Or maybe Tyler was back from Canada and on his phone. Sam sighed as he put on his shoes. They weren't even halfway through their time on Rock Island, and horribly, secretly, he kind of wanted to go home.

When they got into town, Dad headed down to the docks for fish, and Sam, left to his own devices, wandered aimlessly, unsure of what to do with himself. Town was busy, with people bustling in and out of the few stores and wandering through the farmers' market set up by the bank. All around, tourists were clogging the sidewalks, taking photos of the old-fashioned buildings.

Sam's phone buzzed. It was Dad, saying he was going to visit with Captain Jim for a bit and Sam could join them when he got bored with wandering.

Sam sighed.

"You're one of the Fletcher boys, aren't you?" a man asked, as Sam stared wistfully into the window of the bakeshop.

Sam jumped a little. "Huh? Oh. Yeah, I am."

Chase Kark stood in front of him with his big wooden easel under his arm. He smiled, his giant teeth gleaming in the sun.

Sam blushed a little. "Hey there. I still have your change." He felt through his pockets. "I think I left it at home, though. Sorry."

"Pshaw!" Kark said, waving a hand dismissively. "I'll stop by sometime and get it. Not to worry."

Sam couldn't help thinking that if he had thirty-seven

dollars in change waiting for him he'd want to get his hands on it, but he guessed being an adult was different.

"Are you enjoying the island?" Kark continued. "It's . . . well, it's a glorious place. Truly amazing. I'm so inspired here! There aren't enough hours in the day to paint." He gestured wildly with his arm, as though to encompass the entire island.

Sam nodded. It was pretty, he guessed. He just wished he had more friends here. For the first time, being the oldest felt lonely.

"Well, I need to go," he said, starting to walk away. "Have a nice day."

"Where are you heading next? I'll walk with you," Kark said, falling into step next to him. "I'm headed down toward the docks to paint, but a walk would be nice."

"I've got to get . . ." Sam paused. He didn't really know where he needed to go, but he didn't feel like talking to Chase Kark in his bright green shorts. Before he could think of a good excuse he heard his name and looked around gratefully, hoping for a savior.

"Sam! *¡Hola!* How are things?" It was Valerie, waving her big full-arm wave as she crossed the street. It looked, Sam thought, like she was trying to guide in an airplane.

He sighed. "Hey there. What are you doing in town?" It wasn't quite the rescue he had had in mind. In a contest between Valerie and Green Shorts Man, Sam supposed she'd win, but not by a ton.

"On my way to the theater improv group. I film their stuff, remember?" She adjusted her huge hat and checked her phone. "I'd better go! See you!"

Sam gave a slightly panicked look at Kark, who was standing, waiting. "I'll . . . um, I'll go with you. Check it out." He blushed and avoided looking at Valerie.

Mercifully, she didn't seem to find it the least bit odd that he'd suddenly decided to come to a theater group. She just clapped her hands and started walking. "Excellent! They'll be glad to have someone new. But we gotta go. They've already started!"

Sam fell into step quickly. "Okay. Um . . . bye, Mr. Kark!" he called. "We have to go!"

Kark beamed. "Enjoy! Sounds like great fun! All the world's a stage!" His voice trailed off behind them.

"What is he even talking about?" Sam muttered, trying to keep up with Valerie. But she was racing ahead.

"Just have to go to the bathroom. It's right through there," she said, ducking in through the side door of the old United Church. "See you in a minute!" She disappeared down a hallway.

It was cool and dim inside the church entry, and through the doorway Sam saw polished wood and whitewashed walls. It all looked very solemn and important.

"Can I help you?" a voice asked from behind him.

Sam jumped. "Oh! Sorry! There's an improv group, but I don't—" he babbled.

"Oh! You want the Actors' Project. They're this way." The man, who was dressed in everyday clothes except for his collar, gestured behind him toward a hallway.

Unsure of what else to do, Sam followed. The hallway at least looked normal and less fancy, with a worn-out tile floor and plain walls covered with posters and notices. The man opened a door.

"Ta-da! The improv group," he said, clapping Sam on the back. "Have fun. These guys are a riot!" With that, he shut the door behind Sam, leaving him trapped.

"Oh good! We need another partner. You're with me!" Before Sam could duck back out, a tall guy with a stubby beard and a huge grin grabbed him.

"I'm Ted. That's Julia. You're with us. Have you ever done the bench game?" Ted talked fast, and moved even faster. Sam barely had time to register the curly-haired girl named Julia, who gave him a cheerful wave, and the rest of the kids standing around the room in groups of three or four, before Ted jumped into the middle of the room.

"The bench game! We sit on a bench, doing an invisible activity, until one of our partners comes along, sits next to us, and changes the activity up. Then you follow their lead. Nicole, why doesn't your group go first?"

Nicole turned out to be a tall blond girl wearing a Boston Marathon T-shirt. Like Ted and Julia, she looked like she was in high school or maybe even college. Flashing a big grin that showed her dimples, Nicole sauntered silently to the middle of the room, then sat down on the bench. Without saying a word, she mimed putting a key in the ignition, buckling a seat belt, then driving. Every once in a while she'd turn around as though saying something to people in the backseat, and once she took her hand off the (imaginary) wheel to flail and slap at whoever was back there, which made everyone laugh. Val, who had slipped in without Sam noticing, laughed louder than anyone else.

"Okay, Grace, you go! Mix it up!" Ted called after a minute.

Another girl walked forward and took a seat next to Nicole on the bench. Without saying anything she leaned down, pulled out an imaginary phone from an imaginary bag, and began what was clearly an angry conversation. As Grace started doing this, Nicole abandoned her driving role and stood up, pretending to read a book while holding on to a pole on what Sam assumed was a swaying subway car. Every few seconds she would glance up from her book and glare at Grace, shooting her a nasty look, and then go back to reading. Grace immediately followed her lead on the subway car, lurching and occasionally jostling Nicole as though the train were moving.

"And, Mateo, join in!" Ted called.

The game went on and on, and when it was Sam's group's turn he found that it was easy enough to fall in, to remember some of the improvisation drills they had done in the school play rehearsals. Julia went first, pretending to be sitting at what was clearly a very fancy tea party, her pinkie finger extended, her back ramrod straight, as she sipped and nibbled. When Sam joined her, he slouched onto the bench, stretching his legs as far out as he could without falling off. He scratched his head and examined what was under his fingernails, which made everyone laugh. Then he leaned across Julia as though to grab something to eat, and shoved it toward his mouth, chewing with his mouth wide open and pretending to talk at the same time. He kept going, pretending he was a glutton at a feast, grabbing and eating and occasionally offering a huge, silent belch, which got more laughs. Julia followed along, pretending to fight him for food he was grabbing, wiping her mouth with the back of her hand, and even raising partway off the bench as though to let out a particularly big fart. Sam almost burst out laughing at that, but he kept in character, keeping the game going, until Ted joined them and turned them into little kids waiting for their mom.

"And that's a wrap!" Ted called, and everyone burst into laughter and scattered cheers, Sam included.

"That was awesome! Nice road rage, Nic. And, Grace, excellent obnoxious subway rider," Ted said.

Grace, the girl who had been pretending to talk on her cell phone, rolled her eyes and shook her head sadly.

"Dude. Where did you grow up, on a farm? There's no cell phone reception on the subway. I was on a bus. Obviously!"

Sam looked down at his sneakers. He had thought it was a subway too. But Ted just laughed. "You say farm, I say Los Angeles. . . . Whatever it was, you guys were great." He turned to Sam and shook his hand. "And you! Nice work. Love the realistic belches you got in there! Clearly a talented young man."

Sam laughed. "Thanks, I guess."

"How long are you here for?" Julia asked. "We meet twice a week for improv, and on Saturday we do a thing with younger kids outside near the docks, where we pass the hat at the end for tips. You should come out sometime." She was glugging water from a bottle, and when she finished she gave an impressive burp. "That was just for you," she said, laughing and pointing at Sam.

"I'm here until Labor Day," Sam said. "I'll come back sometime, for sure."

"You can always get a ride with me," Val added. "The babysitter brings me in most of the time."

"Excellent," Ted said. "And it's great you're here all month. Most of these clowns are only here for a week or so"—he made a sad face that most of the kids imitated—"but I'm here all summer, working at the Rock Island Actors' Project production for the season. So are Jules and Nicole. Do you do any acting at home?"

Sam shrugged, a little embarrassed. "Not really. Well, I was in the school play last year."

"Oooh, what play?" Julia asked.

"*Annie*. I was Daddy Warbucks," Sam answered.

"Fun! Too bad you didn't get here earlier in the season. We're doing *A Midsummer Night's Dream* for our summer show. But you could volunteer backstage if you're interested."

Sam shrugged again, but he couldn't help grinning. "Maybe. Yeah, I'd actually really like that. I'll have to ask my parents, but probably."

"Cool! It'll be great to have more help." Ted turned away and clapped his hands. "Okay, next one! Let's do the hot lava game! Get in pairs!"

The next game involved all kinds of jumping, rolling, and pretend-falling, and Sam caught on fast. Summer soccer had kept his muscles strong, and he raced around the room, following Ted's bellowed orders: "One foot! Now the other! Now hobble like you're ancient! SOMERSAULT!"

They had just collapsed into an exhausted heap when the door opened and an older man flew into the room.

"Ted! Julia! Crisis time! Can you wrap this up?" the man asked, barely acknowledging the group of panting, laughing kids on the floor.

Ted looked at his watch, then nodded. "Yeah, we're pretty much done. Okay, guys! Grab your stuff, and,

Mateo, don't forget your ugly-but-clearly-special-to-you Giants hat like last time. I can only bear to rescue it once. See you all Thursday, I hope!"

People stood up slowly, chattering about beach plans, what ferry they were leaving on, or the day's games. Val hung out by the door, packing up her bag.

Sam stood awkwardly. He wanted to thank Ted and Julia for including him, so he edged closer, but the man they were talking to was speaking fast. He sounded upset and was pulling at the sides of his hair like he wanted to yank it out.

"—and there's no way she'll come back after the surgery. She's going to fly home to North Carolina, leaving us with no Puck, and without a Puck we have no play! The one role with no understudy! The only one! I can't . . . I don't even . . . Ugh!"

"Is there anyone we can move to that role? One of the fairies or players?" Julia asked.

"Possibly, someone with a small role who could do both. Or one of the lovers, who *do* have understudies," Ted said.

But the man shook his head miserably. "No one else in the company has the making of Puck. We need someone who can do all the physical humor, as well as act. Cam and Derek, and Maia and Georgia, for that matter . . . they're not exactly Puck types, wouldn't you say?"

Sam started to walk away. Clearly this wasn't the time

to interrupt. But before he could leave, Julia glanced over at him. Her eyes lit up.

"YOU!" she shouted, pointing at Sam. Ted and the other man swiveled their heads to stare at him. Val glanced up from her phone.

Ted's face split into a big grin. "Of course! Puck wandered in here around half an hour ago! How did I not notice?" He slapped his forehead. "Sam, meet Alan, director of our modern version of *A Midsummer Night's Dream*. How do you feel about mischievous, troublesome, and ultimately awesome fairies?"

Chapter Eleven

IN WHICH FALLING OUT OF A BOAT HELPS A LOT

Dear Frog, HI!!!!!! Do you like this postcard? It is from a tall hill in San Francisco. We went down it in a cable car and Sara almost barfed. I miss you. Love, Ladybug!!!!!!!!!!!!!!!!!!!!!!!!!!!!!!!!!!
(Mom says that is all the exclamation points I can write.)

Frog Fletcher
Rock Island

"Eli? ELI! Will you help me?" Frog's voice was muffled in Zeus's fur as he struggled to hold the wriggling cat.

Eli didn't move.

"ELI!" Frog shouted, before dropping Zeus. Quickly seizing the opportunity for freedom, Zeus slunk under the couch.

"Rats! Now I can't reach him," Frog said, stomping on the floor in frustration. "And all because you won't help. I needed HELP." He stomped again, but Eli didn't even look up.

Frog walked over to him. "What's wrong? Why are you so grumpy?"

Eli scowled and didn't answer. Frog saw through the screen door that Papa was outside pulling the life jackets and paddles out of the shed.

"Oh! Are you and Papa going kayaking? Can I come? I love kayaking with Papa! He always makes it splash on me," Frog said, forgetting Zeus, who had not reappeared from beneath the couch.

Eli shrugged. "I don't care. I don't even want to go." His shoulders slumped. "I still hate it."

"Why are you going then?" Frog asked. "Papa and Dad always say we have to try something five times before we can say we don't like it, but you've tried it lots of times now."

Eli looked even grimmer. "I asked Papa to take me. I really want to kayak out to Tuckernocket and see the seals. And I want to name the seal in the marine sanctuary."

Frog stared at his brother. Eli's face was pinched and angry, and even with his summer freckles he looked pale and miserable. Frog felt bad for him. Kayaking was so fun! The boat tipped side to side, just a little, when Papa paddled, and it was so nice and low to the water that Frog could dangle his hands in as they floated along. Sometimes the water was so clear he could even see crabs and fish below.

He thought for a minute. "What's the scariest part?" he asked. Frog knew what it was like to be scared. He was scared—really scared—of loud noises. He loved to look at fire trucks and to see police cars flashing their lights, but he hated the noise they made. He even hated fireworks if they were too loud! They made his head hurt and always seemed dangerous, no matter how many times Dad and Papa told him they weren't. But kayaks? What was scary about them?

Eli shrugged. "I don't like how they wobble." His voice was flat.

"Why?" Frog asked. "It's scary when the ferry wobbles, because if you fell out of the ferry you'd be dead, I think. Or really badly hurt. But the kayak is right in the water, down low!"

Eli didn't answer. Frog went on. "Maybe it's like when I was scared of the toilets that flush without me touching them. It just *seems* scary. Remember Dad stayed in with me and we watched it flush again and again, and then it wasn't so scary? Now I can go in those bathrooms anytime and I'm not even scared!"

Eli looked up. "What's your point?" he asked, sounding annoyed.

"Well, I thought maybe it wouldn't be scary if you wobbled a lot and even fell out, because you're so close to the water," Frog said. He was excited. "Can we try it today? Can we?"

"Can we try what, Froggie? Are you coming with us? I told E-man I'd take him out for a paddle. Maybe this will be his lucky trip." Papa smiled.

"Yes! I want to sit in the front of Eli's kayak, not yours. Okay?" Frog asked, bouncing.

"I'm not sure that's a good idea, buddy," Papa said, holding out a hand to pull Eli up, and putting his other hand on the bouncing Frog's head. "You're a lot like Tigger, full of bounce. In the kayak, Eli might not like that."

"But it's like the flushing toilet!" Frog protested.

Papa gave him a strange look. "I don't know if I want to know how they connect," he said, "but I don't—"

"It's fine," Eli said. He was walking slowly behind Papa as they wandered down the empty road to the cove. "Whatever. Let's just do it."

Papa glanced at Eli but didn't say anything until they got to the water.

"Okay, here are your PFDs," he said, handing them the life jackets. "It looks like a lovely day for a paddle, so let's give it a try. E-man, if you really don't mind Frog riding with you, he'll sit in front of you, like this." He positioned Frog, who was nearly vibrating with excitement, into the front of the kayak.

"Frog, NO WRIGGLING. Got it?" Papa said, giving the boat a shove to get them off the rocky shore. "Really. Help your brother out."

Frog nodded solemnly. "Promise," he said.

Eli took the paddle and dipped one end, then the other into the water. They moved forward slowly.

"Cool! I see a school of minnows!" Frog yelled, leaning over the side and peering into the water.

The boat lurched. Eli squawked in alarm.

"Frog," Papa said, paddling quickly up to them.

"Sorry! Sorry," Frog said, straightening up. But there was so much to see! He forgot Eli was behind him, paddling away, and peered around, taking in the cormorants and gulls wheeling overhead, occasionally diving to catch a fish.

"Looking good, E-man!" Papa said. "How is it feeling?"

"Fine," Eli answered, his voice tight.

"Crabs!" Frog yelled, leaning over again.

"Frog!" Eli yelled, swinging his body to keep the kayak level.

"Oops! Sorry. I forgot," Frog said. "But look down. There's a HUGE crab! Bigger than Big Mama last year!"

Eli looked over the edge. The kayak tipped slightly, but he didn't notice. "Oooh! That one *is* huge! I wonder if we can catch it. Papa, did you bring the net?"

"Got it right here," Papa said, reaching between his

feet. He passed the long-handled net to Frog, who leaned over to get it, wobbling the kayak again. This time Eli barely squeaked.

"Can you reach?" Eli asked. His paddle lay across his knees, forgotten, and the boat moved slowly in the current.

"I *think* so," Frog said, leaning over with the net. "OOPS!" The boat swung wildly to the side.

"Careful!" Papa called.

"Don't drop the net!" Eli warned.

Frog leaned down again, but before he could lower the net, Eli yelled.

"Hey! Seal!"

"Where? Where, Eli?" Frog said, dropping the net in his excitement. He pushed forward, looking around wildly.

"Careful!" yelled Papa again.

"Right there!" Eli shouted, pointing. There, barely fifteen feet in front, was a sleek black head, popping up and staring right at them.

"A SEAL! PAPA! A SEAL!" Frog shouted. He swung around, pushing out of his seat. "Do you see? It's looking right at—"

"WATCH OUT!" Papa called. For Frog, while talking, was spinning around in the boat, to better watch the seal, who was clearly watching them.

Eli dropped the paddle as the boat swung wildly. Frog ignored both the paddle and his father's warning.

"Where did it go? It dove down. But wait! It's coming back up over there!" Turning backward in the kayak, Frog pointed behind them. "It's right next to us!"

Eli turned around to see, and for a second the two boys stared at the whiskered face staring at them from just a few feet away.

"IT'S RIGHT HERE!" Frog yelled. Then he fell into the water.

The boat rocked wildly with the impact of his splash, then tipped, sending Eli flying.

With barely a ripple, the seal dunked under and disappeared.

"PHLEW!" Eli spat out a mouthful of salt water as he surfaced. "Where'd the seal go?" he asked breathlessly, shoving his hair out of his eyes and squinting into the sun. "Did we scare it? Shoot!"

Frog, who had already grabbed on to Papa's paddle, pointed with one hand. "Over there. See? It's still watching us!"

"For crying out loud! Can you both please climb back in the kayak? This is starting to feel like an outtake from *Wild Kingdom*. Eli, grab the net before it drifts away!" Papa was holding Eli and Frog's kayak with one hand, and his paddle, which had Frog on the end of it, with the other.

"One second, Papa. Do you think I could swim closer?" Eli asked.

"No. No getting any closer. Seals can bite if they feel threatened," Papa warned.

But no one had told the seal, apparently. It dove, then resurfaced even closer to them, still too far to touch but close enough that Frog could see the patches of gray and black on its whiskered chin.

"It's so cute!" Eli whisper-shouted. "I can't believe how close we are!"

The seal regarded them for another minute, then dove one last time and disappeared. The boys stayed still, treading water and watching to see if it would return. Even Papa sat quietly in his kayak.

Finally the sleek head popped up far away, and Eli let out a huge, happy sigh.

"That," he said, hauling himself up into the kayak and falling into it with an ungraceful thunk, "was the coolest thing to ever happen to me. We swam with a seal!"

"Help me in!" Frog called from the water, where he was trying to pull himself into the boat.

"Come in with me, buddy," Papa said, reaching out to pull Frog up.

But Frog shook his head. "I want to go with Eli. Can I?"

Eli was still staring out at the spot where the seal had disappeared. He turned back to Frog, his wet hair flopping into his eyes and his grin stretching ear to ear. "Sure. Come on up." He reached over the edge, and through some combination of Papa pushing with his paddle and Frog madly pinwheeling his legs, Frog landed in the boat.

"That was really cool, wasn't it? Did you see how close it was? Did you notice its whiskers? It was so cute! I wish I could have one as a pet, don't you?" Frog kept up a steady stream of chatter as Eli reorganized himself in the kayak and took the rescued paddle from Papa.

He started to paddle again, his strokes stronger than before. Frog kept chatting.

"Oh hey! I wonder if that big crab is still here," he said, peering over the side.

The boat leaned sharply as Frog searched, but Eli barely noticed.

"The seal was pretty little," he said. "Do you think it was a juvenile? I wonder if its family is out at Tucker-nocket."

They were almost back at the beach. Papa jumped out and pulled his kayak up onto the shore. Then he dragged Eli and Frog's kayak until it scraped on the rocks.

"Hop out, boys," he said, taking the paddles. "And since you're already wet, want to go for a swim?"

Eli looked down at himself as though surprised to see that he was sopping wet. Frog pulled him toward the water. "Let's swim! Maybe the seal will come back!"

"Coming!" Eli ran past him with a belly flop and a howl.

Frog screeched and followed suit. "Aren't you glad you fell in?" he asked Eli, who was doing a particularly wild series of somersaults in the water. "It's like the flush-ing toilet!"

Papa, who had just waded in to join them, threw his hands up in the air. "Again with the toilet! What am I missing? Why is kayaking like a toilet? Oh, never mind, I probably don't want to know."

Eli splashed him and smiled. "Nope, you probably don't," he said, diving again. When he popped up he swam over to Frog, who was standing in the shallow water, trying to catch minnows.

"When we get home, I'll help you with Zeus, okay?" Eli said.

"You will? Why? You said it was a stupid idea," Frog said, looking up in surprise. He knew Eli didn't approve of his experiment.

Eli just smiled. "I owe you one," he said, and dove down again, leaving only his feet waving against the warm blue sky.

Chapter Twelve

IN WHICH THE PLOT THICKENS

Jax, it is August 15—I'm dating this note because while I believe you are still on the island, that may be wishful thinking.... I don't think we've seen you in a few days. Can you plan to be home for dinner tonight, assuming you haven't left the area code? Alex is welcome to come too. Tell her not to bring any snakes, even the supposedly cute small ones. As we learned at breakfast, Dad isn't a huge fan.

Love, Papa

Jax was, honestly, relieved to get out of the house and head over to Alex's. Now that Sam had to learn a part for some new play in a week, and Eli was all wild to help Frog teach Zeus to swim, Jax was pretty bored at the Nugget. Eli was nagging to do another fund-raising scheme, since they hadn't even made a hundred dollars yet, but the thought of sitting on a hot, crowded street in town asking for more donations was the last thing Jax wanted to do. At least Alex was usually willing to kick the soccer ball around the yard or something.

Of course, it had been a little weird with Alex the first day after the brunch, or Butter Day, as Alex had taken to calling it. After all, did Jax have to say that he had thought she was a boy? Or was that totally rude? He meant it as a compliment, but he wasn't sure Alex would take it that way. Who knew with girls?

Luckily that was the day Alex had found an entire nest of tiny baby mice, so she and Jax started the morning trying to figure out what to feed them, and how to keep them safe from Zeus and Lili. By the time they had relocated the mice to a corner of the Galindo-Greens' massive old barn, Jax had almost forgotten that Alex was a girl.

"Yo, Butter. What's up?" Alex asked as Jax wandered into the yard.

"Nothing. It's so hot today! Are your parents around to take us to the beach? Mine are both busy." Jax rolled his eyes. "Dad has to take Sam into town for his play thing, and Papa is working until after lunch. And it's broiling!" He stared up at the cloudless sky, where the sun was indeed blazing down on them.

"You know what really stinks?" he continued. "We can't go in the lighthouse. It's always way cooler there."

He sighed and stared at the red-striped building, which remained untouched and empty, with the fence still around it. "It's so awesome up there. I wish you could see it." He sighed again.

"Me too," Alex said. She kicked at the ground a little. "It's so lame! They're not even doing anything with it!"

"It would be worse if they were, maybe," Jax said, more miserable by the minute. "They could be working to tear it down right in front of us." His stomach knotted at the thought. He wondered if he should tell Alex about how sad Papa seemed, how Jax had heard him telling Dad that it felt like his anchor to the island was disappearing. "It just really stinks," he repeated, finally.

"We could see if there's a gap in the fence. Have you checked?" Alex sprang to her feet, brushing the dirt off her hands. She had been digging under rocks for salamanders, but it was too hot even for them.

Jax looked skeptical. "I don't know. It's a big fence with Danger signs on it. I doubt it's going to have a hole in it."

Alex shrugged. "We'll never know if we don't check. Let's go!" She started off toward the lighthouse.

Jax followed, moving more slowly. When they got there, they walked around and around the fence, peering at the lighthouse through the metal grid.

"Hey! Check it!" Alex stopped suddenly.

Jax stopped too. On the far side of the fence, away

from the Fletcher house, the gate stood open. Parked inside it, right next to the lighthouse, was a huge, shiny SUV, its gleaming white sides and tinted windows looking bizarre in a place where everyone else's car was coated in sand and dust.

"Let's go in!" Alex said, pushing Jax toward the gate.

"I don't . . . do you think we should?" Jax asked, hanging back. He was torn. There was the lighthouse, open and accessible, but something about that car, and the fence . . . It didn't feel like they belonged.

"It's open. Come on!" Alex ran through the gate, and after a second, Jax followed.

"This is so cool! I can't believe you used to be able to go all the way up!" Alex called from inside the front door.

Jax peered inside. His eyes took a minute to adjust to the dimness of the old building after the bright sunshine. It looked the same as always, with faded plaques listing the names of all the lighthouse keepers, but now the staircase up was barred with a new metal gate and another Danger sign.

Jax stepped inside, where it was indeed cool and comfortable, and sighed. "Yeah, it's amazing up there. You can see Tuckernocket, and the top floor has room for us to put out sleeping bags, or set up a picnic. There are a bunch of other rooms on the other floors, old bedrooms and even a tiny kitchen, but they keep those closed to tourists. . . . You can look in but can't actually go inside them. Still, it was sick." He looked back at the Danger sign. "Hopefully they'll open it up again."

"Hey, what's that guy doing? Is he digging?" Alex stuck her head out the door. "Maybe there's buried treasure here! Maybe some bad guy closed it off so he can dig for the treasure!"

Jax rolled his eyes. "Yeah. I don't think so. That's just the artist guy. Kark." He peered over Alex's shoulder. "But what the heck *is* he doing?"

Chase Kark, once again in his bright green shorts, was talking loudly into a mobile phone that he had pinned between his shoulder and ear while he dug into the hard, dry earth.

"I can't hear. . . . Say it again? What? Can you . . . ? A soil sample. SOIL SAMPLE! Can you hear . . . ? The foundation needs . . . DARN IT." He pulled the phone away and angrily pressed some buttons. Then he looked up.

"What are you doing here?" he asked, dropping the container of dirt. His eyes raked over their faces and dirty clothes. He blinked after a second and smiled. "You're one of the Fletcher boys, right? Well, hello! What brings you here?"

"Just checking it out. What are you doing?" Alex asked, leaning against the side of the lighthouse. "Why do you need dirt?"

Chase Kark's smile grew even bigger. He looked like he

was made of teeth. "Oh! That! Hahahahaha!" He gave a loud laugh. "Just a little . . . well, just an artist's silliness, really. I'm about to start painting and I wanted to really *see* the colors in the landscape." The smile dropped off his face and he looked for a minute like a sad clown. "But enough about that. You really should come away from there. You know I got badly injured by falling rocks. It would be a terrible thing if someone else got injured before we deal with the issue."

Jax didn't like how he said "deal with"—it sounded like he meant *get rid of*. He didn't move. Neither did Alex.

"Where did the stones fall from, anyway?" Jax asked, craning his neck. As far as he could tell, the lighthouse looked as sturdy and solid as ever. Sure, there was some chipping paint and stuff, but nothing really bad.

"Over there. You can still see some of the debris," Kark said, pointing to a pile of crumbled brick and stone. "Now please. You really need to move."

Jax and Alex slowly walked away from the lighthouse. Jax looked at Kark, in his bright white linen shirt and green shorts.

"Where's your painting stuff?" he asked suddenly.

Kark gave them a blank look, then answered, "Oh! It's in the car. I'm driving a bit farther along toward the bluff to paint today. I just wanted to . . ." He trailed off. "Anyway! Can I offer you kids a ride? Do you want to go down to the cove? I'm happy to drop you off." He bustled behind them, toward the SUV.

"No thanks," Alex said. She was standing next to the car, looking at the trunk, which was open. "Cool map."

Jax looked over her shoulder. The trunk was full, but the biggest thing in it was a large poster-board map of the island, with topographical features, model buildings, and a bunch of pins all through it, as well as a leather briefcase, a box of files, and a couple of other containers filled with dirt.

It was cool. Jax started to move closer, but Kark slammed the trunk shut. "Okay! Well, nice to see you both. Now please get back outside the gate. I'll lock it when I drive out. Remember, it's not safe to play here. Have a nice day!"

He delivered all of this over one shoulder while starting the car with a roar, then began to back out of the gate. He waited impatiently for Jax and Alex to exit, then jumped out of the SUV, locked the gate, and jumped back in, roaring down the road with a wave.

Jax watched the dust billow up behind the quickly disappearing car.

"Weird dude," Alex said, wrinkling her nose at the dust. "But at least I got to see inside the lighthouse. Wish I could go up!"

Jax turned to stare back at the lighthouse. With the gate locked again, it looked farther away than ever.

"Come on," he said, starting to walk back toward his house. "Maybe Papa's done working and we can go to the beach."

They walked slowly, the heat draining even Alex's constant energy. They were almost at the house before either one spoke.

"Did you see any painting stuff in the car?" Jax asked.

Alex shook her head. "Nope. Just the map and all the office-looking stuff."

Jax nodded slowly.

"Did you see the lighthouse on the map?" he asked.

Alex paused, then shook her head. "Nope. Definitely not. I noticed because I saw what I thought was our house, but there was no lighthouse, so I figured I was wrong and it was just some other part of the island."

"I didn't see it either," Jax said. "Not anywhere." A strange feeling—half dread, half excitement—was coming over him. He walked faster, then broke into a run. Behind him, Alex started running too.

"What's up? It's too hot to run. Did you hear the ice cream truck or something?" she panted, trying to keep up.

"No. I want to find my brothers. I'm not sure what Kark's really up to. Is he really an artist painting on the island? Why's he always so clean? And why don't we ever see him painting? I mean, maybe he got hurt there, but . . . maybe not. According to the newspaper he was 'checked out by his private physician' but didn't go to the hospital or anything. And if he isn't an artist—"

Alex started to run faster. "Then what the heck is he?" she finished. The two of them ran up the back deck to the house as fast as they could.

* * *

"It's official. Zeus does NOT like to swim!" Eli said, coming out of the bathroom, followed by Frog. "We are not trying that again, okay? We're done with this."

Jax and Alex stared. Eli was red-faced and his glasses sat crooked on his nose. His shirt was soaked, but whether with sweat or water wasn't clear. And he was cradling one arm like he had injured it. Frog didn't look much better. He had a long bloody scratch along his collarbone, which Jax could see clearly through his ripped T-shirt.

"What's wrong with your brothers?" Alex said. She gestured to them. "What did . . . *that?*"

Jax just closed his eyes and shook his head. "Frog has this stupid idea that Zeus can swim—"

"It's not stupid! Felines are natural swimmers! My book says so!" Frog interrupted.

"And Eli decided it would be an interesting experiment in animal behavior to try to train him, and now they're forever covered in fur and water and sometimes blood." Jax finished. "Anyway, we have more important things to talk about. Where's Sam? Don't tell me he's still at that dumb play practice!"

"Call it dumb to my face, fart," Sam said, walking in with a peach in one hand and a bag of chips in the other. "And I'll see how good you look with half a nose."

Jax waved his hands impatiently. "Not now! I need to talk to you guys! Alex and I were just at the lighthouse—"

"Can we get in?" Frog interrupted.

"No! Well, kind of. The gate was open, but that's not the part I need to tell you." Quickly, Jax tried to explain what he and Alex had seen and heard.

There was silence for a minute as everyone digested his story.

"You mean you think he's in *disguise*?" Sam asked. "Like, he's pretending to be an artist who got hit by a bunch of falling rocks, but really he's . . . what? What is he if he's not an artist in bad green shorts?"

"I don't know," Jax said stubbornly. "I know it sounds kind of stupid, but seriously? Think about it. He's got a wicked-fancy car and boat. He must be loaded to buy the lighthouse—"

"Some artists are rich," Sam said.

"Yeah, but remember when we were doing the lobster fund-raiser, we saw him with the town selectmen, and when you saw him in town, and—"

"At Butter Day. Remember, he was at the table at the front," Alex added. "We were introduced to him when Mami and Dad went to say hi to some library people there."

"And his car was all filled with maps of the island and business-type stuff. And what's with the dirt? Why does he need dirt?" Jax went on.

Sam finished the peach and put the pit in the chip bag, which he had also emptied. "You're nuts. It sounds like something out of Shakespeare. He's always putting people in disguises and stuff. Next you're going to tell me some fairy queen is mad at Kark." He started to walk out of the room, but Jax grabbed him.

"No! I'm serious! Something's really weird about this. And just say I'm right. Think about it. . . . I mean, I get it. The federal government is selling the lighthouse, which is awful enough. But this whole might-need-to-tear-it-down thing? That's because it's supposedly so unsafe. But who says it's unsafe! Only he does!"

Sam paused for a minute, then shrugged. "Nope. I think you're nuts. Why would he want to tear it down? *He's the one who wants to buy it!* Did you think about that?"

Jax was silent.

Sam waved his hand. "I don't have time for this." He started to leave again, but turned to look at his brothers and Alex, who were all staring at him.

"Look, I'm as bummed about the lighthouse as you guys," he said, and his voice sounded sad. "But even if you're right and Kark is some kind of lying freak, what are we going to do about it?" He disappeared into the kitchen.

The rest of them looked at each other. Jax almost wanted to cry, he was so mad. How could Sam be so stupid? Didn't he care about the lighthouse? Didn't he care about *them*?

"What's everyone doing in here? I came over to see if anyone wants to go to the beach." Val's voice broke the silence, and everyone jumped.

She stood in the doorway, in her trademark giant hat and with some kind of scarf wrapped around her. Jax was mostly used to her crazy clothes, but today he couldn't help thinking she looked a little like she was wearing a toga.

Alex turned and stared grimly at her sister. "We've got more important things than the beach on our minds," she said. "Jax and I think that Kark guy isn't really some poor artist dude who got hit by falling rocks. We think he's scamming to try to get the lighthouse torn down, but we don't know why!"

Val, Jax realized, was a useful person in some ways. Unlike Sam, she didn't tell them they were nuts. Or look all pathetic and say it didn't matter anyway. Instead, she stared, first at Alex, then at the rest of them, and then she shrugged.

"Okay. Well, I guess you'll need evidence. What do you figure? Try to wiretap his phone? Or should we just follow him?"

Jax blinked. Evidence. Of course! He could have hugged Val, even with her bright pink ruffled bathing suit, flowered toga thing, and giant sun hat.

"I think we should follow him," he said slowly. "That's the best plan. But in the meantime . . ."

"In the meantime let's go to the beach! It's hot!" Alex said.

"We'll make a plan at the beach," Eli echoed, and Frog agreed.

Jax ran to get his towel and boogie board. The lump of dread was fading, and an overwhelming sense of excitement churned in his stomach. Maybe, just maybe, things with the lighthouse could be turned around.

Chapter Thirteen

IN WHICH SPYING IS HARDER THAN IT SEEMS

August 16

To: PapaBear

From: LucyCupcake

Subject: Re: The Lighthouse

Hey, Bro, I can't even believe the lighthouse is still closed! And they might tear it down? Are they crazy? It's such a beautiful spot, it makes my heart hurt to think about it being gone. When will the inspectors make their decision? You'd think that the artist who's buying it would try to get some grants or something to fix it, if it came to that. That's what I would do, at least. I'm going to see what I can find out from here. . . . I'll keep you posted. It just makes no sense!

XOXO Lucy

Eli's brain wouldn't turn off. It felt like someone was playing Ping-Pong in there. Sometimes he was sure Jax and Alex were nuts, and that they'd been spending too much time in the sun. But then he'd look up at the lighthouse and think about it being sold—which, if Captain Jim was right, didn't necessarily mean they would lose it—or, and this was the horrible part, about it getting torn down because it was unsafe, and his stomach would clench. He couldn't help wondering if Jax was on to something. But Sam was right. If Kark was going to buy it, why would he want to do all this safety stuff except to keep it safe? Could he be tricking everyone?

But why? That was the question that always left Eli back at square one. In all the mysteries he'd ever read, it came down to *motive*, to some reason the bad guy wanted to commit the crime in the first place. Why would weirdo Kark want to buy a lighthouse just to ruin it? He didn't live near it, didn't have a house next door or anything. What was it to him? Eli racked his brain, but couldn't think of a reason. Maybe it was some ancient family feud. Maybe his ancestors had been lighthouse keepers and the town did them wrong. Eli shrugged. He had no idea. Hopefully, Operation Guava, as they had named the spying plan, would work. Eli wasn't sure why *guava*, but Alex said it was a fruit that was almost the same color as Kark's shorts, and the name had stuck.

"Are you ready? Come on, if you're coming with,"

Dad said, sticking his head out the back door to the deck, where Eli was pondering the lighthouse.

"Coming!" Eli said, springing up.

His father looked at him, perplexed. "Explain again why you all want to come into town while Sam has rehearsal instead of going to the beach? Jax looked downright cagey. What's going on?"

Eli shrugged, trying not to meet Dad's eyes. "Nothing. We're going to do another fund-raiser. You know, for the lighthouse." This wasn't a total lie. Frog had painted a bunch of rocks and large clamshells with pictures of the lighthouse, which, thanks to its distinctive red-and-white stripes, was easy to identify. The boys planned to ask Captain Jim if they could put them up for sale next to his stand on the dock. Of course, after that, they were hoping to get a glimpse of the elusive Kark and follow him.

"Okay, then," Dad said. "Climb in the van." He went around to the driver's side, while Eli slid in next to Val and Alex in the back, and Jax and Frog sat in the middle.

They were puttering up the winding road, just past the turnoff to the cove, when a shiny white SUV whizzed past them and turned onto the cove road.

"Hey!" Jax yelled. "Hold on!"

Dad slammed on the brakes. "What's wrong?"

Jax whispered, "That was *him*!" Raising his voice, he said, "Um . . . I changed my mind. I really don't want to go to town. I want to get out and go to the cove. Please,

Dad! I won't swim, I promise. I'll just look for shells and crabs and stuff."

Dad started driving again. "Are you nuts? We're heading into town. You can go to the beach later."

"NOOOO!" Jax bellowed, and Dad slowed again.

"Tom, I don't feel very well. I think I'm carsick. I'm going to need to get out," Val said from the back.

"Valerie, I thought you were filming the rehearsal with Sam. What in the world . . . ," Dad started, but a car behind them beeped and Dad jumped.

"For Pete's sake," he muttered, putting on the blinker and easing over to the side of the road. The other car swung by them, with a wave from the driver.

"NOW," Dad said. "What on earth is going on?"

"We just don't want to go to town. It's too hot! Please!" Jax, Alex, Eli, and Val all started to complain at once.

"I need to get to rehearsal. Can we just GO?" Sam asked, looking exasperated. His phone gave a ding. "Hey! Do I actually have service here?" He began texting madly.

"I'll stay with them, Tom. I already have my Red Cross babysitting certificate," Val said. "And I can miss the rehearsal. It's optional, really. Today is mostly blocking and stuff, so I don't need to be there."

"I thought you didn't feel well—" Dad started, then jumped when Sam's phone let out a chicken squawk. "Oh, whatever. All right. Everyone out. CAREFULLY. Frog, you stay with me. We can drop off your painted rocks and get ice cream while Sam has rehearsal. Now, cross the road carefully, and stay together. And DO NOT, under any circumstances, swim."

Dad was still talking as they piled out of the van and slid the door shut.

"BYE, DAD! LOVE YOU! SEE YOU LATER!" Jax yelled as they crossed the road.

Eli glanced behind him as the group headed down the cove road. Dad was staring after them, looking utterly confused.

"Do you think he suspects?" he asked, panting as he tried to keep up with Jax and Alex. Val had stopped to hunt for raspberries a little ways back.

"Suspects what?" Jax asked.

"Well . . ." Eli paused. He agreed it was unlikely that Dad was going to connect their sudden change of heart with the car that passed them on the road.

"I think all your dad is going to suspect is that you've gone nuts," Val said, catching up to them. "Jax, you sounded like a total maniac."

Jax looked a little embarrassed. "I couldn't think of anything to say," he mumbled.

Alex shrugged. "Whatever. We got out. That's what's important. Val, you have your phone, right?"

Val gave her sister a look. "*Mira*. What do you think?" she asked.

Eli agreed that it was a stupid question. Val *always* had

her phone and was usually filming anything and everything with it, narrating as she went.

"Okay, well, I think we need to get close to where he is, then kind of pretend to be taking photos while secretly filming him," Alex said.

Eli was about to speak when they rounded the corner to the beach. Kark was nowhere in sight.

They all paused. "Where'd he go?" Jax asked. The white car, still as shiny as ever despite the dusty dirt parking lot, was right in front of the path to the rocks. But Kark was nowhere to be found.

"Huh. Well, maybe he's on the rocks or something," Eli said. His heart sank. Suddenly the whole spying plan seemed ridiculous. The guy was probably just painting some stupid picture and here they were—with the Galindo girls—making fools of themselves. With a grunt of annoyance, he headed toward the water to look for crabs.

"Hey! Quick, he's coming!" Val grabbed Eli and pulled him toward the dune grass. "Jax! Alex! Come here!"

They ran to the edge of the parking lot, where beach roses, dune grass, and the occasional raspberry bush grew in a thick tangle.

"It's prickly," Alex complained, but she pushed her way into the grass and crouched down.

"Um . . . we aren't supposed to be in here. There are ticks and things—" Eli started, but Val shushed him.

Chase Kark was walking toward his car, talking on his phone. With him was another tall white guy, who looked totally out of place in dress pants and a blazer.

"Can you hear me? This island! No phone coverage anywhere. This stupid beach is one of the only places my phone works at all, and even here . . . Can you . . . ? Good. Anyway, tell me how quickly you think you can get the specs? Uh-huh, uh-huh. Well, the meeting is two weeks from Friday. Should be wrapped up by then. Meanwhile, what are the renderings looking like? They need to be perfect." Kark opened the car and gestured for the other guy to get in.

"Hello? Are you still—? Darn it!" The call apparently failed, and Kark shoved the phone back in his pocket.

"Phone coverage on the island is appalling. Come on, I'll show you the site," he said to the man in the car, and, with a puff of dust from their tires, they were off down the dirt road.

Eli had barely moved, trying to stay hidden until Kark was out of sight. But suddenly his foot burned with a sharp sting. He glanced down, then looked again, in horror.

"RED ANTS!" he shouted, trying to jump backward. Unfortunately, Alex was right behind him, so all he managed to do was to fall into her, knocking her into the thorny edge of the beach roses.

"OUCH!" she screamed, as dozens of tiny thorns grabbed at her.

"Get them off! Get them off! They sting!" Eli screamed even louder, tumbling out of the bushes.

The two of them half ran, half fell from the brush, with Jax and Val close behind them.

"Go rinse them off! Go drown them!" Jax was yelling, pulling Eli toward the water.

The ants had panicked right along with him, it seemed, and were climbing wildly under the edges of his long shorts and up his legs.

Eli stopped to swat them, but they clung to his hands. "GET THEM OFF!" he screamed again, then threw himself—sneakers, shorts, and all—into the water, submerging himself up to his waist.

The rest of the kids stared at him from the water's edge.

"Are you okay?" Jax asked finally.

Eli nodded. With as much dignity as he could muster, he stepped out of the water. "I'm fine. They just . . . sting. That's all."

His sneakers made a loud squishing noise with every step. He paused to try to adjust his leather belt, which he realized with a pang was probably ruined.

Alex gave a quiet snort. "You . . . um. You had ants in your pants," she said, trying to keep her face blank.

Eli just looked at her.

Jax covered his face with his hands, muffling his laughter. Eli turned his glare on him.

"It's not funny," Val started, but her face looked like

she was trying not to laugh too. "*Pobrecito*. Look at all those marks! Are those from the ants?"

Eli closed his eyes for a second, then opened them. He looked down at his dripping legs and shook his head. "No. Those are from the cat. We were trying to teach him to swim."

Val looked at him for a second, then started to giggle.

"Sorry! I'm sorry! I can't . . ." She gasped. "No, really! Just give me a second. . . . I just . . ." She waved her hands, unable to keep talking.

Eli grinned. "It's okay," he said, plopping down on the wet sand. He looked around. Kark was gone, and the conversation they'd heard was totally pointless. He began to laugh too, until tears threatened to pour down his cheeks.

"What?" Jax asked, laughing. "What's so funny? ELI!"

But Eli couldn't answer. The laughter was almost turning to tears. Eli just shook his head, trying to catch his breath. He couldn't really explain it. This was easily the weirdest summer ever. Mostly that felt kind of awful, but just now, just for a minute, it was all okay. Taking a deep breath, he shook his head again.

"Never mind," he said finally. "As long as we're here, let's look for crabs."

Chapter Fourteen

IN WHICH IF ALL ELSE FAILS, TRY THE INTERNET

August 18
To: LucyCupcake
From: PapaBear
Subject: What are you up to??

I ran into Carol from the town council and she said you had called her to ask about the layout and dimensions of the lighthouse's interior. Carol was going on and on about your famous cupcakes and how you babysat her daughters years ago, and she didn't seem to know why you were asking. She might trust you, but I know better. . . . What are you up to?

Whatever it is, I can't wait to see you. . . . Just over a week till you get here! Hard to believe how fast the summer is going. I wish we could grab on to time and hold it still. Not always, mind you. For instance, this morning, when Jax spilled his milk three separate times, then was so busy apologizing and laughing and trying to clean up that he knocked his peanut butter toast onto Sir Puggleton. . . . Well, I don't need to freeze that moment.

XO Bro

"What's up, Froggie? You look bummed," Sam said, coming into the living room. He had just gotten back from rehearsal and pizza with the cast, and was due back at the theater at eight that night for more rehearsals. The play was two weeks away and it was totally coming together. It was kind of awesome to be doing another play, especially one with grown-ups and serious actors and stuff. Julia and Ted, from the improv group, were both in it, and even though they were older—Ted was a high school senior and Julia was in college—they were totally cool, including Sam when they were running lines or just joking around. Sam kind of hated to admit it, even to himself, but hanging out with them at the theater was turning into one of the best parts of the summer.

Frog scowled. "Everything's wrong. Jax and Eli are always off with Alex, you're always at the play, and I didn't get to teach Zeus to swim. And I was so sure he would like it." Frog pushed out his lower lip and crossed his arms over his chest.

Sam regarded his youngest brother with a pang of guilt. It was true that this summer wasn't like others.

Of course, not having the lighthouse was the first—and worst—change. But having the Galindo girls next door was another one, and Sam was secretly relieved that Jax had someone else to hang out with. And of course the play was different too. Sam felt bad for Frog. . . . Everything was changing, and Frog hated change.

He thought for a minute. "Well, maybe Zeus is too old to learn a new trick, but what about Lili? Maybe she'd be more willing to try it. She's likely to try anything!" Lili the kitten remained as wild and unpredictable as ever, often clambering to the high open beams in the living room and dropping down onto the couch with a loud thud, or hanging from the window screens like some kind of demented bat.

Frog just shrugged, his lip pushing even farther out. "Eli quit helping, and then Dad and Papa said I had to stop. I thought Zeus would be a better swimmer because he's older. Lili's too crazy."

Sam put an arm around Frog's shoulder. "Well, maybe because she's crazy she'll like it more. I tell you what, if Dad and Papa say it's okay, we can do a little online research and try to teach Lili. Just to see. But if she hates it we give up, deal?"

"Deal!" Frog's face exploded into a big jack-o'-lantern grin, and he ran toward the deck. "I'll just ask Dad! Then we can start! Okay? I love you, Sam!"

Sam watched him run off, feeling pretty good. He had

to admit that he didn't mind all the changes this summer, but seeing Frog so bummed kind of ruined it. Hopefully they'd have better luck with Lili, and Frog would be his usual happy, totally wacko self again.

The family, including Jax and Eli, who had returned from another unsatisfying morning spying mission while Dad bought groceries ("Kark just walked around town saying hi to everyone! Like he's running for mayor or something!" Eli complained), headed off to the beach.

The waves were perfect, long and straight and curling, and Sam caught a bunch of epic rides on his surfboard before a wipeout filled his hair, nose, and bathing suit with so much sand and salt water that he decided to take a break. The boys lay on their towels, watching people pack up and leave as the sun got lower and lower in the sky. The air was still warm, the late-day sun baking the sand as the beach emptied out around them.

Eli rolled over with a sigh of contentment. "This is the life! Seems like we've always been rushing around this year. We haven't had dinner on the beach practically at all."

"Remember last year?" Jax asked. "We ate dinner here almost every night for a week when Lucy came. And we also played a ton of soccer at low tide. We haven't done that once!" He paused. "Though I guess having Alex playing in the yard so we can do a real two-on-two—no offense, Frog—is pretty cool. Still, we haven't played any beach soccer."

Sam sighed. It was true. Their stay on Rock Island was already half over and it seemed like they had barely done any of their usual stuff.

"At least we're here today," Dad said from his chair. He was reclined all the way back, his face tilted up toward the sun. "Let's enjoy what we *are* doing and not worry about what we aren't."

"And remember, every summer is different," Papa added. He was lying on the blanket with a towel over his face, but he was still listening. "Remember a few years ago when it rained for three weeks of the month? Or the time, Eli, you had terrible ear infections and couldn't get your head underwater? Or when we all got that stomach bug—"

"UGH. Let's not relive that summer. I'd like to repress all memories of it," Dad interrupted.

"You get the point. We remember the good parts, but problems happen, and changes happen too, whether we want them or not. This summer has a lot of good things."

Eli shrugged. "I guess. But I still miss the lighthouse."

The others nodded.

"Me too," Papa said. And his voice was a little sad. Dad patted his hand.

"Well," Papa said, after a minute, still beneath his

towel. "We have almost two weeks left. The lighthouse might not be a sure thing, but what else do you guys want to do? We should soak it up and make every moment count! Let's make a list, and we'll check off as many things as possible."

The boys started shouting out their ideas.

"Bike to Gilly's!"

"Eat dinner at the Sisterhood!"

"Have another lemonade stand!"

"Buy a book at Rock Island Bookworks!"

"Kayak to Tuckernocket!"

"Teach Lili to swim! Sam is going to help me, right, Sam?" Frog added.

The rest of the group groaned.

"Sam, save yourself and refuse. Seriously, take it from me. I bear the scars of one who has learned the hard way," Eli said, holding up his scratched and scarred leg.

"And I bear the scars of one who just keeps getting mauled for no reason!" Jax added.

Sam shook his head, smiling. "A promise is a promise. Besides, I'm not messing with Zeus. He's practically as big as I am. No, we're going to try Lili. She's such a wing nut, she might just love it."

Eli looked at him pityingly. "You just keep telling yourself that," he said. "But Dad, you'd better buy more Band-Aids the next time you're in town."

The sun dipped lower in the sky, and Dad looked at his

watch, sighing. "Well, lads, I'm afraid it's time to pack up. We have to get home and eat so that Sam can head in for rehearsal."

The group started to groan, but Sam stood up, grabbing towels and throwing them into the beach bag.

"Blegh! Sam, shake the sand off *away* from people. Especially people like ME!" Papa said as sand flew everywhere.

"Sorry! But let's go," Sam said, grabbing his shoes.

Jax glared at him. "You're in a hurry," he accused. "Since when are you so psyched to leave the beach?"

Sam just shrugged. He wasn't about to tell Jax that rehearsal was one of the most fun parts of the day.

"I told Frog I'd look online for tutorials on teaching cats to swim. Let's roll," he said, grabbing his surfboard.

"I'm telling you, you're nuts," Jax grumbled, but he picked up the cooler and started toward the car. "What's the play about, anyway?" he asked.

Sam walked quickly, his mind racing with thoughts of the play. So far he was loving Shakespeare way more than he thought he would. There were more jokes, and more downright funny parts, than he had expected. But his role, Puck, was the coolest. He was a fairy, which sounded kind of lame, but was actually awesome. He was all action and trouble, leaping and rolling around, like gravity could barely keep him down. And the guy who played Oberon, the fairy king who was Puck's master, was this huge guy named Carl with a big beard who looked almost scary and was totally believable as someone who would boss everyone around. The whole thing was cooler and more exciting than Sam knew a play could be.

"Well, it's about this fairy queen and king who are in a fight. And then there are these four, like, older teenagers, called the youth of Athens, or the lovers, and they're all messed up. . . . One guy likes a girl who likes him back, but the other girl likes him too, and—"

"Skip that part," Jax interrupted. "Go on about the fight."

"I'm a servant of Oberon, the fairy king, and he has me get a plant that makes a person fall in love with the first thing he or she sees. He wants me to sort out the lovers so they all like the right person. But then, since Oberon is mad at Titania—she's the queen—he has me use it on her so she'll fall in love with some weirdo. And last, there are these, well . . . kind of loser country-bumpkin guys, and they're putting on a play. And they're hilariously bad. But then we enchant one of them so that he has a donkey's head, and he's the one that Titania falls for."

Sam paused.

"Anyway, it's all mixed up and crazy and everyone is with the wrong person and freaking out. By the end, Puck sorts it all out, and everything's right in the world again." He fell silent.

Jax digested this for a second. Then he shrugged.

"Cool, I guess," he said, and turned to Eli, begging him to join him and Alex for flashlight tag later that night.

"Are you thinking about Lili?" Frog asked Sam in the van as they wound their way to the house.

Sam turned to look at Frog, who was wrapped in Jax's sweatshirt in the back. Frog's eyes were bright and excited.

Sam smiled. "Yep," he answered, lying a little bit. "As soon as we get home I'll do some research and we'll get started tomorrow."

Frog's face fell. "Not tonight? Why not tonight?"

"Well, I have play practice, and—" Sam started.

"But not until after dinner!" Frog said. "I heard Papa say he'll take you after we eat! Can't we start tonight?"

Sam glanced out the window, where the light had turned a glorious orange as the sun sank almost to the horizon. The day had gone by so fast! He sighed, then smiled.

"Sure, Froggie. We'll get started right away," he said.

Eli shook his head. "Wear protective gear," he said. "Trust me. You don't want to do this."

But Sam just grinned. "Sure we do, right, Frog?" he said.

Frog beamed.

Chapter Fifteen

IN WHICH ELI'S BIRTHDAY STARTS WITH A SPLASH

August 19

Dear Eli! HAPPY BIRTHDAY! It has been quite a year for you, what with trying the Pinnacle School, researching yurts with Anna, and now—if rumors are true—kayaking out to Tuckernocket on your birthday! I'm so proud of you, nephy-poo! As proud as Aunt Marge was of Dudley Dursley, and for far better reasons. You are growing into such a brave, curious, interesting person, and I am glad to know you. Can't wait to hear about the kayak ride.

XOXOXO Lucy

P.S. I might be bringing four new flavors of cupcakes to the island. There might be caramel in three of them. XO L

Eli couldn't sleep. It was his birthday tomorrow. Well, today, really, since it must be after midnight. Eli had celebrated every one of his birthdays on Rock Island—the only Fletcher boy to do so—and while he sometimes wished he was home with his friends, he mostly loved the birthday rituals they had here. Like Papa and Sam going into town early in the morning to pick up fresh blueberry muffins, still hot from the oven, and then . . . But Eli shut his thoughts down, or tried to. Because then they'd take the muffins to the top of the lighthouse, and Papa would take a photo of them all, marking their heights against the stone wall, checking how much they had all grown that year.

Of course this year would be different. They couldn't get into the lighthouse, and despite a week's worth of spying, they hadn't gotten any incriminating evidence against Chase Kark. They had seen him on the dock, driving his fancy boat up to a mooring near Captain Jim and rowing himself in to meet with a bunch of old men, but he hadn't said anything suspicious, at least nothing that they could hear from their hiding spot near the bait buckets. And then Captain Jim's assistant, Charlie, had nearly poured buckets of fish guts and blood on them when he was cleaning out the fishing boat, which was possibly the grossest thing that had ever happened to them. And they had seen Kark again when they were picking Sam up from rehearsal, this time standing near the bank with three men in suits and briefcases who looked very out of place on the island, but that time he had given his big clown smile and cornered Dad for ten minutes to chat, asking about their summer vacation and what Dad had been reading lately. The boys had escaped into the theater, which was really just the back of the church, figuring even Shakespeare was better than Kark.

Eli sighed and rolled over. Then he rolled over again. Finally he sat up and looked at the clock. It was almost five in the morning. Already the barest hint of dawn was brightening the sky. Soon it would be his birthday! Lying back down again, he closed his eyes, willing all bad thoughts of Kark and the lighthouse away, trying to dream of seals and soccer games, bridges and building forts with Teddy and Jamil at home, until he drifted back to sleep.

"Is he ever going to wake up? I'm hungry!" Frog said from the top of the ladder.

Eli opened his eyes, bleary and disoriented. He had been dreaming, dreaming hard, about a school in the woods where he had to fight to find food. Now he was awake, his stomach grumbling. Outside, Sir Puggleton was barking.

"What time is it?" he asked, squinting toward the clock. "I was awake half the night."

"It's almost nine o'clock! And we have muffins! And SOMETHING ELSE!" Frog announced importantly. "I thought you would never wake up!"

Eli jackknifed out of bed. "Nine? Why didn't anyone wake me! Let's go!" Grabbing his glasses, he started to race downstairs, but Frog put up a hand.

"Wait! I have to announce you!" He turned down the ladder and bellowed, "HE'S AWAKE!!! HE'S COMING!"

Eli cringed. Frog at his loudest was really, really loud.

"Thanks, buddy, we got it," came Dad's voice from downstairs.

"I'm pretty sure the Galindo-Greens got it too. Probably the Harringtons heard it over by the cove," Sam said. "Jeez, Frog, could you be louder? Please?"

Frog ignored him and climbed down, with Eli close behind.

"HAPPY BIRTHDAY!" chorused Dad, Papa, Sam, Jax, and Frog. They were standing in front of a pile of presents, and Eli was sufficiently distracted by the size and lumpiness of the pile that he didn't notice Frog inching toward the deck.

"Frog!" Papa said sharply. "Hold up." He turned back to Eli. "Normally we would have breakfast first, then presents, but we have something very special today, and it can't really wait. So . . . outside you go!"

Eli cast a longing look at the muffins, but he was too excited to care that much about leaving them behind. With a few big steps he was through the living room and at the door to the deck. He stared out, unsure what to think.

Captain Jim and a college girl whom Eli vaguely recognized from Sam's play were on the deck, with a giant plastic kiddie pool between them. And in the pool . . .

"A SEAL!" he yelled. "That's a seal!"

"Very good!" Jax said. He turned to Sam. "I thought he was supposed to be so smart. Wow."

Eli ignored him and stepped forward. The seal was tiny, not much bigger than Sir Puggleton, with a sleek black head and enormous eyes. Its mouth was open in what looked like a smile, and it was splashing about the pool like it was having a ball.

Captain Jim swept one arm forward, like he was presenting royalty. "This here is our little rescue pup from the marine lab. Julia, who's an intern there this summer, was going to help me bring her back out to Tuckernocket today, because she's old enough to survive on her own. But we thought you might want a birthday visit before she goes. And after all, once you make your birthday trip out there, you get to name her."

Eli plopped down on the deck and kneeled next to the pool. The little seal was nosing a plastic toy as she scooted around in the water.

The other boys crowded around, only stepping back when the little seal splashed a huge wave of water at them.

"What do you say, E-man? Is that a pretty cool birthday visitor?" Dad said.

Eli nodded. "I can't . . . It's the best thing in the entire world!" He felt like his face would explode from smiling.

Captain Jim smiled too. "I'll tell you, we wouldn't take a detour like this for just anyone. But I've seen you kayaking around out there, brave as can be, and, well . . . eleven years old. That's worth something! Happy birthday, Eli."

Eli couldn't speak. He was so happy. Happy to be eleven, happy to be brave enough to kayak, happy to be sitting with a seal on Rock Island. He reached out a hand, then pulled it back.

"Can I . . . Am I allowed to touch her?" he asked.

Julia stepped forward. "Sure, just be very gentle. In fact, you can give her a fish if you want." She reached into a cooler next to the pool and pulled out a small piece of fish. "Just be careful—she can take a chomp without meaning to! Throw it to her and see what she does."

Eli flung the piece of fish high in the air, and they all laughed as the little seal leapt up and caught it.

"What are you going to name her? What? Will you name her Ladybug? That's a nice name, don't you think?" Frog asked, clapping his hands in delight.

Eli shook his head. He had been thinking about the name ever since Captain Jim first mentioned the seal and had finally decided. Before he could tell them, though, the phone rang in the house.

"That's going to be for you, E-man," Dad said, walking

back inside. "But I'll tell them you're busy visiting with a seal. I'm sure whoever it is will understand."

Eli threw another piece of fish to the seal. She let it fall into the water, then pushed it up with a flipper, catching it as it flew upward. Once she had swallowed she turned toward Eli and gave a loud, honking bark.

"She wants more," Julia said, laughing. "She's a little piglet, this one. Here, Eli, one more before she's all done."

Eli took the fish from Julia. He thought that being an intern in the marine lab for the summer was about the coolest thing he could imagine. Maybe when he was older he could do that! The thought was tantalizing.

"So? What's the name going to be?" Sam asked. "How about Puck?" He grinned at Julia, who grinned back.

"I think a version of *A Midsummer Night's Dream* with seals would be spectacular. We just have to get Alan and the rest of the cast on board," she said, laughing.

Eli shook his head. "Nope. I decided on the name a while ago. I'm going to call her Anna. For my friend Anna, who lives on a farm in Maine," he told Julia and Captain Jim. "She's already named a baby goat after me, so it's only fair. Besides, Anna is a nice name for a seal."

"Anna the seal . . . I like it," Captain Jim said, nodding. "It suits her, and it will wear well." He clapped his hands. "Well, Anna, how'd you like to get back into the big lake? Time for a real swim, don't you think?"

The little seal stared up at him, then took a flipper and splashed with it, hard, so that Captain Jim, Julia, and Eli were all covered in water.

Eli scrambled backward, laughing and wiping water from his eyes.

"What was that for?" he asked.

"She's just telling us she's getting restless, that's all! Time to get rolling." Captain Jim turned to Julia. "Let's get her back in the truck. I'll pull around and you can get her cage ready."

Within a few minutes Captain Jim and Julia had coaxed Anna into the truck bed, where she quickly galumphed her way into a large cage. Julia rewarded her with another piece of fish.

"Well, Team Fletcher, why don't you give us a half-hour start, then set your kayaks for the island? We'll get Anna settled and meet you there. You can help with some fieldwork—you know, counting the pups and that sort of thing. Sound good?" Captain Jim asked from the driver's seat.

"Sure! We'll be there," Eli said, his eyes on Anna. She was contentedly nosing a ball around the cage, ignoring the idling of the loud engine.

Dad had come back out, and was talking quietly to Papa. But he looked up and answered quickly, "Of course!

Wouldn't miss it for anything. Thank you, Jim, truly. This was a real treat for the boys." He smiled, but Eli thought he looked distracted.

"Who was on the phone?" he asked Dad. "Is something wrong?"

Dad shook his head. "Not at all! I'm great! It was Lucy, but I told her we'd call her later. Can't wait to hit the water with you, E-man! Let's get some breakfast . . . those muffins have been waiting!"

They waved goodbye to Captain Jim and Julia, then trooped back inside. Eli's insides felt like a low-burning campfire . . . all warm and bright and cozy. He was aglow with the fact that he was on a first-name basis with a creature like Anna. Rock Island felt more magical than ever, and he had a moment of feeling sorry for his brothers, whose birthdays would never be in such a special place.

"Her first name is Anna, but maybe you guys can choose her middle names," he said expansively, through a mouthful of muffin. "Maybe she's Anna Ladybug Puck . . ." He turned to Jax. "What name do you choose?"

Jax spoke quickly. "Frost. You know, like in *X-Men*."

"Okay. Anna Ladybug Frost Puck. It's a pretty good name!"

The other Fletchers agreed, and for the rest of breakfast, the tearing of wrapping paper, and the phoning of grandparents, Eli kept the warm glow, knowing that soon they'd kayak out and see Anna again.

* * *

The kayak trip to Tuckernocket was easy, Eli thought, as he paddled home in the fading afternoon light. They had spent the whole day there with a picnic lunch that included birthday cake and salami. Eli had used a clipboard and a data sheet to track the approximate ages of all the seal pups born there that spring. Then they had collected shells; Eli found a piece of dark blue sea glass, and Frog found a tiny perfect starfish. It had been the best day ever.

As he paddled home, his hands stinging slightly with newly formed blisters, Eli stared at the shore of Rock Island, lit up in the afternoon sun. The lighthouse stood like a beacon, guiding them home. He felt sure they would be back inside before too long. On a day like this, anything felt possible.

"Dad, can we ask Captain Jim or Carol or someone about when they're deciding on the lighthouse? I can't wait to hear—I have this feeling we're going to be allowed back in! It's weird, I know, but I just have a feeling."

Dad, who was paddling next to him, didn't answer right away. Eli looked back at Tuckernocket, almost invisible now, then back toward the lighthouse.

"Dad?" he said again. "Will you?"

With a few strong strokes Dad pulled slightly ahead, and Eli could barely hear his voice when he answered.

"Sure, E-man. But for tonight, let's just celebrate. Eleven years old!" He turned briefly in his kayak and smiled at Eli.

"Happy birthday, son. I hope it's a great year."

Eli smiled back. He was sure it would be.

Chapter Sixteen

IN WHICH SAM WON'T WEAR A WIG (BUT ZEUS WILL)

Your play sounds SO cool! I can't believe you're doing Shakespeare. Text me as soon as you get your costume—I can't wait to see what you're wearing. You are so lucky! I've got a pretty sweet princess dress for these fairy tales, but I bet you have something completely awesome. I'm jealous! Em

Sam was pretty psyched with the way the summer was going, all things considered. He had gotten some sick surfing in, and was going to save his money to buy a new surfboard next year. His brothers were willing to play soccer almost every morning, so he was in good shape for the Shipton Elite team. And the play, which he would NEVER have thought he'd do, was turning out be the best accident he could imagine. Shakespeare, it turned out, was a pretty funny guy. There was a character in the play called Bottom, and there were tons of silly, gross jokes and stuff he never would have thought would be in a play with all that *thee* and *thou* language.

Plus, he got to hang out with the older kids, like Julia and Ted. Ted was hilarious—for sure one of the funniest people Sam had ever met. He cracked them all up constantly in the part of the bumbling country bumpkin who thought he was a great actor. Julia was funny too, but she also had a kind of coolness to her that made it hard to watch anyone else when she was onstage. She played one of the "youths of Athens" who got mixed up in the fairies' tricks, falling in love with the wrong guy and getting lost in the woods. The whole thing was cool to be a part of. And here, on Rock Island, Sam didn't have to worry about fitting the play in around soccer practices and homework, let alone having Tyler or some of his other friends bugging him about being arty. Here, he could just enjoy it.

"Big day, Sammy! You ready for your costume?" Julia asked when they were at the theater for evening rehearsal.

Val was there too, of course, faithfully filming, and Sam had to admit that she was part of what made the rehearsals fun. Unlike his brothers or Alex, she actually cared about the play and was always laughing at the theater jokes that his family didn't understand. Sam realized that despite the crazy scarves and ruffly bathing suits, Val was relatively normal. It was weird to be so comfortable with such a girlie girl . . . he guessed it must be like having a sister. Brothers he knew *all* about, but Val was definitely different.

"I wonder what you'll wear," she mused, perched on a stool next to the light table, her knees drawn up to her chin. "There are so many cool ways to do Shakespearean costumes. And since Alan is doing this one as a kind of modern take, set in the woods of New England with a big businessman as the duke . . . well, it could be really fun!" She sighed. "I wish I could design the costumes! I have lots of ideas."

Sam and Julia looked at her. Val was wearing some kind of orange-and-red-print long shirt thing, with a head scarf and dozens of wooden bracelets. Sam laughed.

"I'm sure you do, but I'm not sure I'd want to wear your costumes. Nothing personal, of course."

Val made a rude gesture, but she laughed too. "Oh, nothing personal, but I would rather eat a bug than walk around in the endlessly boring little-boy T-shirts that you wear. So we're even."

Julia gave Sam a look. "You do dress kind of like a four-year-old," she said. "I think my little brother has those shorts."

Sam looked down at his shorts. They were normal black sport shorts, though he had to admit they were a little frayed. And maybe getting a little small. Still, who cared? It was summer! He was about to say so when Alan came out on the stage and clapped his hands.

"Okay! Is everyone here? Terrific. We're going to pass out costumes now, but I'd like you to wait until the end of rehearsal to try them on, complain about them, or anything else you plan to do, got it? We have around ten days until showtime, so let's not waste time. We'll start with the nobles: Lysander? Helena? Come on up."

One after another, the cast members jumped onto the stage and grabbed their costumes. Everyone laughed when Teddy picked up the donkey head and pretended to give it a long, passionate kiss.

"Puck! Come and get it!" Alan yelled, toward the end of the cast list. "We had to change it slightly. . . . The kid who was going to play Puck was a lot smaller than you, Sam. But I think it will work."

Sam ran up to the stage, a rush of anticipation in his stomach. He loved this part, the moment when the costumes changed them all from a bunch of everyday people saying lines into someone totally different.

"Um . . . are you sure this is mine?" he asked, when Alan handed him a series of hangers and turned back to his list. "This looks . . ." He trailed off, unwilling to say more.

Alan glanced up distractedly. "What? Yes, of course I'm sure. Oberon! You're next!" he called, dismissing Sam.

Sam climbed down from the stage, his heart sinking.

He couldn't wear this! There were purply-rose velvet short pants . . . he thought they were called knickers. And a silky, puffy shirt that looked like it belonged on a pirate. But the worst part by far was the curly blond wig, complete with a flower wreath in it. It looked like something one of the tiny china figurines his grandmother had lining her mantel would wear . . . not something a hard-core, athletic, totally wild fairyland creature would be caught dead wearing.

Alan clapped his hands again. "Okay! Remember, no complaints or comments. Let's jump into it. I want to get back to act three, scene one. Places!"

Everyone scattered, and Sam slunk over to his spot on the stage. This was one of the more complicated scenes, in which the various mortal lovers wake up and Oberon realizes that Puck has messed up and given the love potion to the wrong boy. Normally it was one of Sam's favorites; he had to dance around Oberon's temper while keeping his mischievous attitude of not really caring what happened to the dumb mortals. During the scene he got to leap off some of the stage scenery and climb various ropes, but today he didn't even want to move.

They went through the scene, with Alan barking at Sam practically every other line. Finally Alan called a halt.

"Sam! What's going on with you? Are you not feeling well? This scene is you at your most manic. . . . Puck is excited by the trouble he can cause and desperate to prove himself to Oberon, his master. Why are you phoning it in?"

Sam's face burned. Ms. Daly would never call someone out like that. He was humiliated. Visions of the velvet pants kept popping into his head. "Sorry," he mumbled.

"Let's try again," Alan said, and they did.

But Sam didn't find it any easier this time. Finally Alan called a halt. "Go take a break. Get some fresh air or something. Let's move on." He shot Sam a look. "You be sure to get a snack. I need more from you than that." He turned back to the other actors, and Sam trudged out of the theater toward the break room, where they kept a supply of cookies, grapes, and popcorn.

At the end of rehearsal the others chattered about their day and the costumes, throwing out questions and laughing, but Sam stayed silent. Clearly no one else was being a baby about the costumes. Of course, as far as he could tell, no one else was wearing weird velvet knickers and a pirate shirt. He felt sick to his stomach. He couldn't complain about his costume, could he? Not with this group of serious actors, all buzzed and ready to go. He felt like a total fake.

Sam hid the costume in the car that night, not wanting to deal with it. But the next morning he brought it out to show his family. He hoped that it would look better with fresh eyes, but instead it was worse. The wig was a terrible sight—bright and fake-yellow, with big pink roses woven through the curls. Sam held it up at breakfast.

"See what I mean? It's awful, right? I'm not just making this up. It's really, really bad! I just . . . how am I supposed to play the role dressed like this?" He shook the velvet pants.

Sam's brothers and parents stared silently at the costume. Sam was gloomily satisfied that they looked as horrified as he felt. Papa, in particular, was incredulous.

"What the heck?" he asked, tentatively touching the wig, then pulling his hand away as though it burned. "I mean, if you're going to rock a wig, it should at least be a *good* wig."

Sam flapped his hands impatiently. "What does it matter about the quality? It's hideous! I can't wear it! It has nothing to do with Puck, the way I imagined him. And . . ." He trailed off. "Everyone else is older than me, and no one else is complaining or anything. So I don't know what to do."

He flopped face-first onto the couch, which was gritty with sand, as usual. The Nugget had sand everywhere, all summer long, no matter how often Papa bellowed at them to rinse off in the outdoor shower before coming inside. Sam shifted uncomfortably.

Jax poked at the wig, then shook his head, in clear

disgust. "You can't wear that! There's no way! Right? Dad, Papa, you'll talk to the director, won't you?"

Dad sat next to Sam on the couch and pulled him into a one-armed hug. "I wish I could, but I think this is something Sam has to deal with on his own. He's right—no one else is going to have their parents complaining about their costume. I think this is one of those times we can't really do a whole lot." He leaned back and looked at the costume again, lying on the back of the chair where Sam had left it. "It certainly is a disaster of a costume!"

Sam was ready to quit the play. This was NOT what he had signed up for. If there were photos of him in that wig . . . He shuddered.

"Well, at least—" Eli started, but before he could finish, Lili came tearing into the room from Dad and Papa's bedroom, with Zeus close behind her, his bushy tail streaming out in a gray streak.

"Watch it!" Jax yelled as the cats raced across the coffee table, launched themselves into the air, then landed, one after the other, on the kitchen counter. "They're nuts!"

This, unfortunately, was nothing new. "The witching hour," as Dad called it, came over them frequently, and they would leap from the sleeping loft, race through the house, and generally cause mayhem and anxiety.

Lili gave a weird yowl and jumped off the counter onto the dining room table. She stopped short, regarded the costume for a second, then launched herself at it. Zeus followed close behind.

"Get off! Get them off!" Sam yelled, trying to extract himself from Dad's hug and the squishy couch cushions.

"Lili! Stop that!" Frog yelled. He reached for the kitten, but she had tangled herself deep in the synthetic blond strands of the wig, rolling and snarling it around her claws. She yowled and Zeus flung himself on her, whether to attack or rescue her, it was unclear.

"NO!" Sam yelled. As bad as the wig was, he didn't want it mangled! Alan had already lectured them all about the theater's shoestring budget and how they couldn't afford any extra expenses.

"Get the cat treats! Quick!" Eli yelled, following his own orders and running for the kitchen. Sure enough, when he shook the jar of treats both cats froze. "Come on, Lili-cat," he cooed. "Time for a treat."

Lili looked up at him, her green eyes almost hidden by the now chewed and frizzy nylon strands of the wig. Carefully, Eli moved in and untangled her.

Sam picked up the wig. "I can't . . . What the . . . What am I supposed to do now? Look at this thing!" He shook it.

The family regarded the wig in silence. It had gone from looking like an ugly wig to looking like . . . well, like something the cat had chewed up and spit out.

"I'm going outside. I can't deal with this." Sam flung the wig down and ran for the door. He didn't know whether to laugh or cry. On one hand, the wig was now completely ruined, so he didn't have to wear it. On the other . . . he had to explain *that* to Alan, and somehow he thought the whole "the cat ate my wig" story was unlikely to cut it.

He nearly slammed into Val and Alex, who were walking up the yard.

"Whoa! What's wrong?" Alex asked. She was holding a bucket. "We came to see if you wanted to walk the road with us. The blackberries are *insane* right now! But you look like you're going to kill someone."

Val gave him a sympathetic look. "Is this about the costume? I could tell it wasn't really what you had in mind. I don't blame you. . . . I've never seen a Puck who looks like that. Especially a boy Puck. I wonder if the person who was going to play the part was a girl."

Sam shrugged. It didn't really matter at this point. He had a lame costume and a ruined wig, and somehow he had to make them work.

"You know, I once read an awesome book about a boy who traveled back in time to Shakespeare's day and actually met and hung out with William Shakespeare, and they acted in *A Midsummer Night's Dream* together," Val said. "And Puck wore body paint and weird antennae and looked really cool. I wonder if Alan would be interested in that."

"Probably not," Sam said gloomily. "He already chose the costumes. And he's not about to change them just because I say so."

"Well, maybe *I'll* say so," Val said, undaunted. "Because your costume now is a nightmare."

Sam shook his head. "Just leave it," he said. He didn't want to make it worse.

"Why shouldn't I at least ask?" Val said, hands on her hips. "If there's one thing I've learned with Mami, it's that the squeaky wheel gets the grease. What's the worst Alan can do to me? Say no? Tell me I can't film the production?" She shrugged. "Puh-lease. He needs me to film it if he wants it to be shown on the local cable access channel."

Sam couldn't help being impressed by Val's boldness.

"If . . . well, if you don't mind, that would be cool. I mean, I guess it can't hurt," he said.

"Val will boss *anyone* around," Alex said, shoving her sister lightly. She looked a little proud. "You should have heard her yesterday. We were trying to listen in on Kark and those suit guys—who are still on the island, by the way—at the Sisterhood. And this big group of day-trippers came in and sat between us and them, and Val totally asked them to move." She shook her head. "It's a little scary. You're as bad as Mami."

Val seemed unconcerned. "You need to go after what you want in this world. I want to make movies, which is my long-term goal, and I want to know what that weirdo is up to on this island! Dad's been talking about this place forever, and we haven't been here since we were babies, and now all of a sudden this Kark guy is going to buy the lighthouse and it might need to be torn down? I don't buy it." She scowled.

Sam couldn't help laughing. Alex laughed too.

"Okay, Sherlock," Alex said. "You keep trying to solve the mystery. In the meantime, Sam, tell those guys to come on already! I want those blackberries!"

Chapter Seventeen

IN WHICH THE SPIES GET BUSTED

August 24
To: PapaBear
From: LucyCupcake
Subject: Just doing a little research
Hey, Bro,

I'm not telling you anything yet, but I'll just say that the thought of the lighthouse being torn down because the town can't raise the funds is NOT okay by me. One thing all these years of working in New York has taught me is that there's more than one way to skin a cat. No offense to Lili or Zeus. I'll keep you posted. I can't wait to get there. Elon too. . . . He's been hearing about it forever. Elon and Rock Island . . . it's going to be interesting!

XO Luce

Jax was bummed. They had just over a week left on the island, and they hadn't gotten anywhere. Eli kept nagging them to do another fund-raiser, but so far the lemonade stand, the lobster races, and the painted rocks had earned ninety dollars or so. It was a ton of money, if they had it to spend, but nothing compared with what they'd need to save the lighthouse. It hardly felt worth it. Not only was the lighthouse still closed but a bunch of workers in big trucks had come out and done all kinds of surveying and measuring, though what they were measuring was unclear. Still, it made Jax nervous.

"Maybe they're just measuring what would be required to fix it," Alex said hopefully.

Jax and Alex were back in town, wasting a perfectly good beach day wandering up and down Main Street, hoping to spot Kark and his minions, as Eli had taken to calling them. Eli wasn't with them. When Jax had refused to do another lemonade stand, Eli had gone off kayaking with Papa to do "fieldwork" on Tuckernocket. Jax figured that meant he counted seals, and it was an excuse to give up spying, but Papa and Dad were so glad Eli liked kayaking that they were happy to go along.

"Maybe. But I don't trust them. Hey! Is Val coming to meet us? I wanted her to try to film them, if we find them," Jax said, craning his neck.

Alex shrugged. "Who knows? She was off to go boss around the director of the play. She said she'd try to find us but not to wait."

Jax was about to say something when Alex grabbed his

arm. "There he is! Come on!" She started down the street toward town hall, where Kark was standing, once again in his terrible green shorts, with a group of men in suits.

Jax and Alex reached the wide stone steps just as the men disappeared inside.

"Darn it," Jax said, breathing hard. The building looked serious and official, with big stone letters and a plaque on the wall.

"Well, come on! Don't stop now," Alex said, starting up the steps. She was dressed, as usual, in sports shorts and an oversized Chicago Bulls T-shirt, her short hair hidden under a ball cap.

Jax glanced down at himself. He was a little dirtier than usual; they had stopped to pick more blackberries on the way into town, and he was stained with blackberry juice and, unfortunately, a bit of blood where the thorns had scratched him.

"Can we go in? I mean, dressed like this?" he asked, hanging back.

"Of course! It's a public building," Alex said, opening the huge door.

Jax shook his head, but followed. The Galindo girls were nothing if not bold. He wondered if that came with living in so many foreign countries. Maybe he would be bolder if he hadn't always lived in Shipton. He doubted it. Jax hated getting in trouble.

"There they go. Let's follow. But . . . slowly, like we're

just hanging out," Alex said, heading down an empty hall.

Jax looked nervously around. Doors with signs like WATER AND SEWER and TOWN CLERK lined the hallway, and inside the rooms people were hard at work, typing on computers and talking on phones. No one looked up as he and Alex walked past.

They moved silently down the carpeted hallway, toward the doorway at the far end, where Kark and his companions had vanished.

When they got there, Jax saw the sign. LAND USE AND PERMITS. Outside the door, which was open a crack, they paused, listening.

"Well, of course we need to see what the surveyors say. It's our fervent hope that they think the lighthouse can be saved! Of course. But if they feel it's unrealistic . . ." Kark's voice trailed off. "I just wanted to find out about a contingency plan. Strictly a plan B, obviously. We're all hoping for the best possible outcome."

Someone else said something about "maintaining the historic character and ensuring that the site has new life," but Jax couldn't quite hear the rest. The room was noisy, with a clanking air conditioner and a ringing phone.

Jax and Alex edged closer.

"Mostly we just want to ensure that the pieces are in place so that, if the worst-case scenario *does* happen, we are able to move quickly on mumblemumble," Kark said, his voice smooth and soothing.

"What's he saying?" Jax whispered. "I can't hear him."

Alex slid one Converse-sneakered foot into the doorway and nudged the door open, ever so slightly. Jax held his breath.

"Unprecedented, of course," said another voice, "but we feel mumblemumblemumble."

Jax was getting frustrated. Was this the secret? They needed to hear! He moved against Alex's shoulder, pressing closer.

With a crash, they both fell against the door, slamming it open.

"WHAT THE—" Kark yelled, jumping back as Jax and Alex fell into the room.

Jax tried to stop himself from careening forward but only managed to grab on to the edge of a desk—and the leg of the person next to it—as he fought to keep his balance. The man whose leg he grabbed leapt backward, but Jax held on, trying to pull himself upright.

"HEY! Get your hands off me!" the man bellowed, shaking his leg and glaring at them. He felt in his pockets. "You were going for my wallet! Nice try, punk, but that's not going to work on me. Someone call the cops! I didn't think we'd have to deal with *this* kind of urban problem on Rock Island."

The guy behind the desk looked young and scared. Jax vaguely recognized him from around town. "Rock Island doesn't—" he started to say, but the older man ignored him.

"I'm using your phone. We need the cops in here!" he said. "Trust me. Best thing to do for these types of kids is to teach them a lesson."

"No, really, you don't—" Jax started to say, straightening up and taking a step forward, but the man interrupted him.

"Stay right where you are. Don't move. Keep your hands where I can see them," he growled, looming over Jax and Alex.

'Sheldon, I—" Kark started to say, but the other man—Sheldon—cut him off. "I got this. We get a lot of this in Miami. Kids masquerading as innocents, sent out to pickpocket or commit other petty crimes. Let me handle it." He shook his head, never taking his eyes off Jax and Alex. "First thing is to keep an eye on them until the police get here. Trust me, these people are usually working in groups."

Jax stared. "Are you nuts? We're just—"

"QUIET!" the man yelled, and Jax jumped. Alex put a hand on his arm.

"Just shut up," she whispered. "He's a freak show. Leave it."

Jax did as she said. His face was burning, and he was glad the ball cap hid his eyes. He was trying not to cry. The man used the desk phone to make a call, staring at them the whole time.

"Now, we'll see if we can get some answers," Sheldon

said after hanging up the phone. "They're sending someone right down. You punks better just watch it. I'm sure you've got all kinds of tricks, but I'm warning you, don't try them here."

Kark shook his head. "This makes no sense." He stared at them, and his eyes bugged.

"Are you . . . aren't you one of the Fletcher kids?" he asked, his voice rising. "What the—? I keep seeing you everywhere! Are you following me? What's going on here?"

"You know these kids?" Sheldon asked, his voice incredulous.

"Yes. He lives . . . well, it doesn't matter." Kark stared again. "And is that . . ." He trailed off, his face blanching slightly.

Alex, who had taken off her ball cap, gave a big, unfunny smile. "Alexandra Galindo at your service. Daughter of Natalia Galindo. We met at the library breakfast, remember? She'll be SO happy you thought I was a gang member!"

At that moment a uniformed police officer walked into the office. Jax was relieved to see it was Thalia Levee, a part-time animal officer who knew Sir Puggleton, and the rest of the Fletchers.

"What seems to be the issue, gentlemen?" Officer Levee asked, her hand resting lightly on her nightstick.

Kark wiped the sweat from his forehead with a big

white handkerchief. "It's nothing, really. We were just . . . surprised by these youngsters, who burst in here rather unexpectedly. I don't think it's a police matter."

Sheldon opened his mouth like he wanted to say something, but Kark shot him a look.

Officer Levee gazed at Kark and Sheldon, then at the young clerk at the desk, who was staring at his hands, then at Jax and Alex. She held their gaze for a minute, until Jax looked down.

"Are either of your parents in town with you?" she asked.

Both Kark and Sheldon started talking at the same time. "There's no need to involve their parents! It was just a misunderstanding," they said, talking over each other.

Alex answered. "Jax's dad and my mom are both here today. We can call them if you want."

Jax wanted to hit his friend. What was she thinking? Dad was going to be so mad. . . .

Officer Levee walked over to the phone and picked it up. "Numbers?" she asked.

Numbly, Jax answered.

They stood in silence in the office, waiting for Dad and Natalia to show up. Twice Sheldon started to talk, but Kark shushed him.

Finally, with a clatter, Dad and Natalia flew into the office.

"What's the matter? Is everything okay?" Dad asked,

sounding flustered. His hair was sticking up more than usual, and he was sweating. Jax ran to him and pressed against his side. No matter if he *was* in trouble, he was glad Dad was here.

Natalia, on the other hand, didn't look frazzled. She looked mad.

"Everything is fine, I think," Officer Levee said. "But I thought we should clear up a few things. Sir, would you like to share your concerns?" She gestured to Sheldon.

He looked hugely uncomfortable. "It's nothing," he mumbled. "They banged into the door and startled us, that's all."

"I believe you were concerned that we were pickpockets or some other criminals," Alex said loudly. "Because *our* kind of people always are. Wasn't that right?"

Kark cleared his throat. "He was . . . mistaken. Obviously. It was understandable—"

Natalia cut him off. "I'm sorry. Why was it understandable? Because when I look at them I see two dirty eleven-year-old kids, not criminals. But since they are not white, perhaps your associate saw something else?" She glared, and Kark winced.

"I . . . That has nothing . . . ," he babbled.

"Really? So if, say, two blond, blue-eyed children banged into the office door you would have assumed the same thing? That they were criminals? You would have called the police? You're certain it has nothing to do with the fact that they're a young black boy and a young Hispanic girl?" Her voice rose, and Officer Levee put a hand on her arm.

The clerk stared. "That's a girl?" he asked, but everyone ignored him.

"Now, let's—" Officer Levee began, but Natalia rolled right over her. She took a step closer to Sheldon. Sheldon was a tall man, and Natalia was short, only a few inches taller than Jax, but she looked like she was going to deck him.

"You realize what's going on here, right? This is outrageous!" she said.

Sheldon fell silent, but Kark began to bluster. "You can say what you want, but those kids have been following me around for weeks and I have to wonder what they were doing outside the door in the first place!"

Jax gulped, and Alex looked at her shoes.

"They've been lurking around my boat, following my car, and generally disrupting my peace when I'm trying to paint! I don't know if their intent is criminal or just mischief, but I've had enough!"

Natalia opened her mouth, then closed it again.

"Kids?" she said, looking over at them.

Dad spoke for the first time. "Jax, do you want to say anything?"

Jax silently shook his head.

Dad stared at him for a minute, then turned his gaze to Kark and Sheldon.

"Well. Whatever the kids have been doing—and I'd like to remind you that they're *kids*—we, as their parents, will handle it. Meanwhile"—he shot Sheldon a dirty look—"I suggest you think long and hard about whom you accuse of being a criminal in the future."

Natalia broke in, taking Alex by the arm. "Indeed. Especially as I have a team of lawyers and publicists that would love to hear about how my daughter and her friend were treated by . . ." She paused. "Who are you exactly, again?"

Sheldon flushed an ugly purple. "Sheldon Drake. Drake Investments."

Kark coughed. "I'm sorry for any misunderstanding on our part. But the larger story—for your *publicists*—might be that these kids are harassing visitors and tourists on Rock Island. So. I think we're done here." He turned his back on them with an air of finality.

"Okay then," Officer Levee said, sighing. "I think that's about it. Gentlemen, have a nice day. I'll walk my young friends out."

She stepped out of the office, and Jax and Dad followed, with Alex and Natalia right behind them.

Alex started to speak.

"DON'T!" Natalia said sharply. "Just don't. I'm too angry to talk or listen right now."

"But Dad—" Jax started.

Dad held up his hand. "We will talk about this at home.

With Papa. What that man . . ." He trailed off. "That was disgusting. I'm just heartsick that this happened."

Natalia shot him a rueful look. "Was that a first for Jax? All over the world, my girls have been stared at, asked to bring cocktail peanuts, or followed by hotel detectives. America's not the worst place for it, but it's not the best either. A new employee in the Chicago office called security when Alex ran in screaming one day. Turned out Val had fallen in the lobby and knocked out a tooth."

Dad looked defeated. "It's not like race hasn't come up before, but we live a pretty sheltered life, I guess. Shipton is an easy place to live, but of course, the rest of the world isn't Shipton." He sighed.

Jax felt terrible. Now that it was all over, the weight of Sheldon's accusations felt embarrassing and gross.

Dad put an arm around him and pulled him close. "We'll talk about this at home," he repeated. "But in the meantime, and I'm sure Natalia will agree, there will be no more lurking around Chase Kark. Trouble like that we don't need."

Chapter Eighteen

IN WHICH THE PUNISHMENT DOESN'T FIT THE CRIME

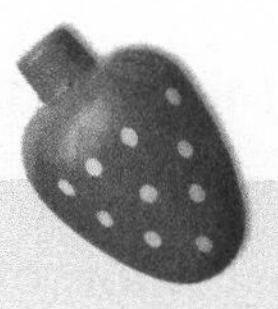

Boys, consider this a benevolent form of house arrest. That means you can hang around inside, outside, or at the Galindo-Green house. It also means you cannot walk down to Cove Beach, spend time alone in town, or be out of sight for very long, lest you be skulking under desks and behind cars on your spying missions. THIS ENDS NOW.

Papa and Dad,
seconded by Natalia and John
(A United Front)

Frog wasn't quite sure what had happened, but everything—and everyone—was weird all of a sudden. Jax and Dad had come home the evening before looking grim and upset, but nobody was talking about what went wrong. At least, nobody was talking to Frog. Jax and Dad and Papa had holed up in Papa's office, where voices had gone from soft to loud, then soft again. Frog had no idea what was going on, but then Dad had come out and told Frog, Eli, and Sam, who was home from rehearsal and jamming a post-dinner taco into his mouth, that whatever spying game they had been playing with Chase Kark needed to end.

Eli had spoken up, explaining their hypothesis . . . at least, Frog *thought* that was what he'd called it: that Kark was a bad man who didn't just want to buy the lighthouse but wanted to have it torn down for some reason. But that just made Dad even angrier, and he went on and on about how you can't accuse someone of things like that and not get in trouble and Eli got red in the face and said that's why they were trying to get proof and Dad got red in the face and said people were innocent until proven guilty, even if they wore ugly green shorts, and they needed to back off. Then Eli stormed outside.

Frog sighed. Sam was supposed to be researching lessons on teaching a kitten to swim, but between all the yelling Frog was sure he'd forgotten. He sat forlornly, wondering what had gone wrong.

"Come on, let's see what we can find about turning Lili into a swimmer," Sam said, suddenly appearing next to Frog in the living room. "We still have over a week left on the island—I bet we can do it!"

Frog leapt to his feet. "Really? You have time?" His

heart lifted. He SO wanted to try to teach one of the cats to swim! He didn't even remember why anymore, but it felt important. Even more important now, with the whole summer collapsing around them—mad brothers and the closed lighthouse and everything messed up and different.

"Sure, buddy." Sam looked down at him, and Frog smiled for what felt like the first time in forever. "Let's do this!" Sam clapped his hands, loudly, like it was a big sports play, then grabbed Frog around the middle and ran around the room.

Frog shrieked with laughter, then, when they had made a full circle, tumbled out of Sam's grasp and back onto the couch. "Let's look! Let's see what it says!" he gasped, trying to catch his breath.

They hung over the kitchen table, where Dad had said they could use his laptop.

"Hmm . . . it says here to get them used to the water with a dripping faucet or a sponge. . . ." Sam kept reading while Frog watched breathlessly.

Sam clicked and read and clicked some more. Frog thought he was just pretending to read, he was moving so fast. But Sam was amazing like that.

"Okay," Sam said suddenly, standing up straight. "Here's the deal. These experts—and they seem pretty smart—suggest we get into the water with her, like in a pool or something. NOT a bathtub!" he added quickly. "She'd claw us to ribbons. But we get in the water, then gently lower her in and support her as she starts paddling." He paused, apparently lost in thought.

"But we don't have a pool," Frog said finally.

"True. But we do have Cove Beach," Sam answered.

Frog considered this. It was very calm there, not that *that* had helped Zeus like swimming. Frog winced at the memory of Zeus clawing his way up and over Jax, trying to get back to his cat carrier.

"Do you think Dad will let us go?" Frog asked. "After all, he said all that stuff about couch arrest—"

"House arrest, not couch arrest," Sam corrected. "Well, I don't have rehearsal until this afternoon, so let's at least ask if he'll take us down there. I'm sure Jax and Eli will want to get out too."

Dad, when approached on the back deck, agreed readily. He didn't seem any happier about house arrest than they were. Jax and Eli, however, were harder to pin down. Jax had gone over to Alex's house, and Eli was up in the loft on his bed, and refused to go anywhere.

"You're cutting off your nose to spite your face," Dad called. "Come on, E-man. Let's get outside."

"I don't need my nose to know that this is unfair, and that we've lost our last shot to know what's really going on with the lighthouse," Eli said. He sounded mad.

Dad sighed, and Frog knew that it was hopeless. Eli got mad and stayed mad.

"Okay, let's head out," Dad said finally, giving up on Eli. "We'll drive. It's easier with the cat."

They were pulling out of the driveway when Val ran up. "I was just on my way over! Sam, I was *finally* able to talk to Alan last night. I told him about my ideas for the costumes. I didn't mention the state of the wig—may it rest in peace—"

"Or pieces," Sam interrupted.

"—but he was definitely intrigued. He seemed kind of distracted, to be honest. But he basically said if we had a better costume to bring it to the rehearsal and he'd see what he thought." She paused and looked into the van. Frog and Lili looked back at her.

"Where are you guys going? Can I come?"

"Hop in," Dad said, sliding open the van door. "We're headed to the cove for Operation Wet Cat."

Val laughed and shook her head as she climbed in. "You are tenacious!" she said to Frog, as she settled next to him. "Can't wait to see how this will go. Good thing I have my camera. Actually, Frog, I have something even better! Hey, Tom, hold on a minute!"

Dad stopped, and Val jumped out of the van and ran back to her house, her floppy beach hat flying off.

"Here," she said breathlessly as she got back into the van, having picked up her hat on the return trip. "Do you know what this is? It's a waterproof video camera you wear on your head. I use it for skiing. But you can wear it in the water and film Lili's attempts."

Frog grabbed the camera and wrestled it onto his head, while Sam turned sideways in his seat to ask Val about skiing. Frog pressed all the buttons he could feel, a few times each, just to see what happened, but nothing changed. He would have to ask Val how it worked. Lili reached out a curious paw, touching the camera once, and Frog bounced with excitement. This was going to be awesome!

Frog barely waited until the car stopped moving before he raced down to the water. Lili was a natural, he thought. Unlike Zeus, she was curious about the water, so they let her bat at it with her paws and splash it before Sam gently lowered her in, keeping the kitten far from his body as he did so. But Lili didn't flail wildly or try to climb back up his arms. She began to move her little paws, tentatively at first, then harder, until she was swimming with just a little bit of help from Sam.

"Can she swim to me? Can she?" Frog was electric with excitement. Lili's orange face was held up proudly out of the water, and she looked, he thought, pleased and happy.

"Let's see. Just be careful. Don't hug her to you, in case she gets freaked out," Sam said. He was grinning, looking almost as proud as Lili.

Frog nodded, and Sam let go, pushing the kitten gently toward Frog. Without the slightest effort, Lili swam toward him while Dad and Val whooped from the shore.

"Okay, head over to the rocks," Sam said. "See if she'll swim over to you."

"What if she gets tired?" Frog asked anxiously. The rocks were pretty far away. It was easy for him. . . . He was a big kid and could walk there over all the rocks and crabs and broken shells. But Lili looked so tiny!

"I'll stay close," Sam promised.

Frog started walking, turning away from Sam and heading around the edge of the cove. The water was higher here, up to his waist almost, but the tide was going out and he could still walk easily enough. From time to time, he bent to watch the schools of minnows swimming around his legs.

It took only a few minutes, but now he was out of sight from Sam, Dad, and Val. Frog looked up at the rocks. There, perched on a high ledge, was Kark's easel. The canvas on the easel was blank, Frog noticed, and the artist was pacing around, talking on his phone.

Frog froze. Was he going to get in trouble for spying? He wasn't even spying! He was swimming! But what would Dad think? He stood still, wondering what to do.

"This bloody island! I half wish we'd stuck with Nantucket. This place is too small, and too backward, to do anything! I'm out on a rock, still with this stupid easel, because there's no cell phone reception anywhere!" Kark ranted into the phone.

Frog closed his eyes, hoping he would stay invisible.

Kark fell silent, and Frog opened his eyes. Had he been spotted? No, the man was just pacing, listening to whoever was talking.

Then he spoke again. "Hah! No, I was only kidding. It's worth it, even with all the provincial yahoos. We're ninety percent there. The inspectors are on-site as we speak, and I have them buttoned up." He paused. "Not to worry. They're airtight. They're not even taking real estimates. They'll go with whatever I give them. It's in the bag. Once I own the land outright and turn in their results that the structure is unstable, there's nothing in the town's bylaws or building codes that states I can't build what I want there, as long as the Coast Guard has access."

He laughed, and Frog thought it was a very unfunny laugh.

"This time next year there will be gorgeous top-shelf condominiums where that broken-down piece of rock is! The Coast Guard can attach whatever they need, but the rest of the land is free and clear. And once the condos are up I don't ever need to come back here. So hang in there . . . we've almost got it. And believe me, with the kind of restrictions they have on building here, we can easily charge three to four million apiece. Easily! Everyone wants in on this place, because it's so 'unspoiled'!" He laughed again, then fell silent, listening.

"A week or less, hopefully. By Labor Day at the latest. I'll keep in touch," he said finally.

Frog didn't wait any longer. Moving as carefully as he could, he turned away from the rocks, where he'd been staring at the pacing Kark, and waded back around the cove to find out where Sam and Lili had gone.

He bumped into Lili, closely followed by Val.

"Sorry! That took longer than we thought. But she's doing so well! I can't believe how much she likes it!" Val exclaimed. "She even tried to catch a minnow! It was the cutest thing I've ever seen!" She gestured toward shore. "There was a bee out there and Sam totally freaked out, so I took over following Lili." She laughed. "Boy, he really hates bees!"

Frog waved his hand impatiently. Who cared about that now? Breathlessly, he told her what he could about the conversation he'd overheard.

"And he said by this time next year the big chunk of rock would be gone! No, wait, he didn't say that exactly. But he said something about combinations being there and millions of dollars!" Frog was near tears with frustration. Why hadn't any of his brothers been there? He couldn't remember the words Kark had used, and he knew they were important.

Val eyed him. "Combinations?" she said.

"Something like that! And he said this place is unspoiled and that's why people would pay millions," Frog went on.

Val shrugged. "That doesn't sound great, but I don't

think we can do anything," she said. "I've barely ever seen my mom so mad. I'm not kicking that hornet's nest unless we have real proof."

Frog shuddered. "Don't talk about hornets," he begged

Val just laughed. "You're as bad as Sam! Listen, bud, I don't think we can do much unless you can remember more."

But Frog stomped his foot, splashing the water. Lili tried to catch the wave as it sloshed her, but Frog barely noticed. "I heard him!" he shouted. "He said the pile of rock would be gone, and that the inspectors were going with what he gave them! Or something like that!"

Val stopped laughing. "Are you sure?" she asked. "You're sure he said that?"

Frog nodded miserably. "I can't remember his words exactly, but he said, 'It's in the bag.' I don't know what bag, though." He paused. "And he gave a mean laugh. Not like something was funny, but like . . . mean." He sighed. He wished so hard that Val had heard it all too.

Val and Frog stood there while Lili splashed around them in tiny circles. It was a gorgeous August day, brilliantly sunny with a tiny cool breeze to remind them that summer was coming to a close.

"Well," Val said finally. "I guess I can try and tell Mami and Dad. They're not mad at me for spying. Or not yet, anyway."

Frog sniffled. “Tell them he said it would be gone,” he repeated.

Val nodded. “I’ll try,” she said. “I don’t know what you heard, Froggie, but it doesn’t sound good. It doesn’t sound good at all.”

Chapter Nineteen

IN WHICH EVERYTHING GOES WRONG, IT SEEMS

Alex, WHERE ARE YOU? Did you guys go off island? Your car is still there but nobody's seen you guys since last night! It's starting to get creepy. If you get this, come over.

Jax

Of course it would rain, Jax thought. It *would* rain during the last week of their vacation, while they were still under house arrest. And Alex and the rest of the Galindo-Green family seemed to have disappeared. Val had been over yesterday, after she and Sam and Frog had taught Lili to swim. Unfortunately, when Frog had taken off the video camera headset it was dead, which bummed Val out, since she had been sure it was charged. But she had shown them the video *she* shot, which, Jax had to admit, was seriously awesome, and had promised to send Papa the link to her finished "film" so they could watch it on the computer. Then she'd gone home, promising Frog—Frog, of all people—that she would talk to him tomorrow. But now it was raining and no one was answering at the Galindo-Greens' place, and Alex hadn't come over as planned, and everything was awful.

Frog was *still* babbling. He had been ever since they had gotten back from the beach yesterday. "You *GUYS!*" he whined. "You're not listening. I heard Kark talking on the beach yesterday! And he's . . ." He paused. "I don't remember what he's doing but he said the lighthouse would be gone next year!"

Sam was at rehearsal, where he had no new costume to show his director, so he had left the house freaking out. Eli and Jax were playing a lackluster game of Connect Four. Jax shifted his weight on the sandy couch. When it rained like this, everything in the Nugget felt damp and sticky, and Jax stared miserably out the window at the lighthouse, which he could barely see through the driving rain.

"Did you hear me? *GUYS!*" Frog whined again.

Jax whirled on him. "We heard you, okay? But what are we supposed to say? There's nothing we can do about it, so why don't you shut up?"

Frog's lower lip trembled. Jax felt like a jerk, but he

didn't care. Things had gotten so bad so quickly! Like pressing a bruise, his thoughts darted back to the scene at town hall, when Kark's weirdo friend had thought he and Alex were some kind of criminals. Natalia's words played over and over in his head, as did Dad's reply: *"My girls have been followed by hotel detectives,"* she'd said. *"We live a pretty sheltered life,"* Dad had answered.

"What's your problem?" Eli asked, putting a red chip in the slot. "You don't have to be such a jerk. And I won," he added.

Jax stood up from the couch, knocking over the game. "My problems have nothing to do with you. NOTHING." He stormed up the ladder and into the loft, where he could be alone. He was mad. Angrier than he could have imagined a few days ago, when he and his brothers and the Galindo girls had been having a picnic on the beach, bodysurfing and digging giant holes, laughing until his eyes streamed tears over Alex's never-ending puns. He gulped and burrowed his head in his pillow until only his ears showed. He grabbed another pillow and pulled it on top of his head. He didn't want to hear or see anything anymore.

Jax had almost fallen asleep when Papa came up and sat on the bed. He gently put a hand on Jax's back.

"You under there somewhere?" he asked.

Jax shrugged, making the pillows move.

"Want to talk about it?" Papa said.

Jax shrugged again. He didn't, not really. He wasn't sure how to talk about it . . . how mad and embarrassed he was, how mad he was at Papa and Dad, because they couldn't possibly understand. Finally he spoke.

"Why aren't there any black people on Rock Island?" he asked. As soon as the words were out he wished he had just shut up. He didn't really want to talk about this. He spoke again, quickly. "Never mind. Forget it."

Papa carefully moved the pillows until he could see Jax's face. Jax tried to look away, but Papa put a hand on his head.

"That's a good question, and a fair one. I mean, there are some folks of color here, but you're right, it's pretty homogenous. You know what that word means, right? It means everyone's alike."

Jax nodded. He wished he'd never said anything. It's not like their family didn't get singled out or noticed. Jax was used to people asking why he had two dads, or why he didn't look like them. But he wasn't used to being looked at like a criminal. And he hated it.

"I guess the real answer is 'I don't know,'" Papa said, and his voice was quiet. "I want to know, but I don't, and I really hate not being able to answer your question. I know a lot about what it's like to be me—to be a white man, to be Jewish, to be gay, to be a dad. But even if I try, I can't really know what it's like to walk in other people's shoes. Not yours. Not black families who choose *not* to vacation here, not that jerk businessman Sheldon's. I'm afraid I'm not much help." He sighed, a big, deep sigh.

Jax felt even worse. He hadn't meant to make Papa feel bad, even if he was kind of mad at him.

But Papa gave his shoulder a squeeze. "One of the reasons we chose Shipton for our home is because there are all kinds of folks there. Dad and I wanted to feel at home, but we also wanted our growing family to feel at home too, and never feel like 'the only ones,' whatever 'one' that might be. But Rock Island . . . well, we never chose it, really. I came here when I was really little, and we just kept returning. It's a pretty special place, and it has a lot of family history. But you're right. It might not be a place that's as welcoming as we'd want."

"I still like it here," Jax said. "I don't want to stop coming. I just . . . wondered. I mean, part of me feels like I belong here, because we've been coming forever. But I don't know." Jax's face started to burn at the memory of the look Sheldon had given him. "Now I kind of feel like I don't belong."

Papa nodded and held him tight. "Figuring out where you fit in the world is hard for anyone, and maybe harder for you than most. But you belong anywhere you want to be, Jackson David Fletcher. You belong on Rock Island, where your great-grandparents came on vacation a hundred years ago, and you belong in the Minority Student Alliance at Shipton High School, when you get there, and you belong at that crazy-loud church that Elon and Lucy brought us to in New York, and you belong in Mimi and Boppa's synagogue, though I admit it's incredibly hard not to fall asleep during Rabbi Belstein's sermons. That man . . . well, that's beside the point. He means well. And the Sukkoth was really cool, at least."

Jax laughed a little, remembering Mimi poking Papa in the back when he had dozed off during services last year. He felt a little better.

"I'm not going to pretend it's easy. Heck, being a human being isn't easy. And you're a young black man, Jax, which means some moronic and bigoted people will make assumptions about you before they know you. As you grow up you *will* face more people who judge you, and I'd be lying if I said skin color doesn't matter. But you have every reason to be proud of who you are and what you look like. And you definitely belong on Rock Island, a place you love and that's in your memories as far back as you can remember. You belong here way more than that slime weasel ever could."

Jax snuggled into Papa. He felt a little better, hearing Papa say those things. Not all the way better, not better enough to totally forget how it had felt standing there, but better.

Papa squeezed him hard, one last time, then let him go. "When you get a chance, talk to Elon about this. He's traveled all over, and he probably has some thoughts about being a black man in the world."

Jax nodded, unfolding himself from the bed. "Can I

ask you one more thing?" he said, heading toward the ladder. "What's Frog talking about? The lighthouse being gone next year? Is he just being his usual weird self?"

Papa looked down at his lap. "I don't know, buddy, to tell you the truth. Frog's story is a little odd, but he doesn't tend to lie."

Jax stared at his father. "Are you nuts? He told people we had a baby brother named *Connecticut*!"

Papa smiled, but it looked forced. "Well, true. But that's different. He makes stuff up, but he doesn't lie." He sighed, a big, sad sigh.

Jax felt cold. "What? What's going on?" he asked.

When Papa spoke, his voice was quiet. "Today's paper had a story about the lighthouse. It seems the foundation, and even the soil beneath it, is very vulnerable. The surveyors aren't sure it can be saved without spending a ton of money. And Kark is getting ready to close the sale, and he was just quoted as saying that he 'would make the best of a difficult situation and leave it to the experts.' "

"What? Says who?" Jax said. His heart sank, and for a second, he felt like he was going to be sick.

"Says the construction and surveying firm that did the inspection. They're a big Boston-based company, and they do a lot of this kind of work. So the town pretty much has to accept their findings." Papa sighed, then stood up.

"Let's go, my son," he said, resting a hand on Jax's head and brushing his fingers through Jax's hair, which was starting to get thick again. "This day is turning into a tough one. Lucy and Elon are coming in tonight on the late ferry, but I think we should head into town early, meet Sam after his rehearsal, and have dinner at the Sisterhood. We deserve it."

Jax paused on the ladder. Part of him didn't want to go back into town, back to where people would be watching him, maybe thinking things about him. But he didn't want to stay here either, staring out the window through the rain at the lighthouse. He was glad Lucy and Elon were coming. Lucy always made them feel better, with her cupcakes and giant hugs. And Elon . . . he was just cool. Jax couldn't help being a little bit excited. Between the cupcakes and the magic tricks, things had to get better.

Clambering down the ladder, Jax saw that Frog, Eli, and Dad were laughing at the kitchen table. Dad looked up.

"Oh good! You guys have to see this! It's hilarious." He moved over to make room for Papa and Jax.

Jax slipped in next to Eli, who scooted over and patted his back as he peered over Dad's shoulder. Jax gave him a smile. "Sorry I was such a jerk," he mumbled.

Eli waved him off. "It's okay. Sometimes I'm a jerk too. Today was just your turn." He pointed to Dad's laptop. "Check this out. Val sent it yesterday, but Dad just opened his email. And no, she didn't say anything about them leaving the island. It's weird. But anyway, you have to see this."

Dad pressed Play, and they all watched a video of Frog and Sam and Lili in the cove. Val had edited it and added a funny, bouncy song about surfing, and the whole thing looked totally professional. Jax couldn't help grinning, then laughing out loud as Val zoomed in on Sam's freaked-out face as a bee buzzed near him. It ended with a wide shot of the cove, the rocks, and the beach around them, looking exactly like a video postcard of Rock Island. The whole thing was just a few minutes long, but it felt like they were watching a real movie.

"Val really is talented. We have to show this to Captain Jim. And frankly, Thalia Levee would love this too," Papa said. "I'll send them the link." He clicked around on the keyboard, leaning over Dad's shoulder, then straightened up.

"Now! Hopefully that helped put a few smiles on some Fletcher faces. Let's take that good mood and head to town for ice cream, Sisterhood, and Lucy!"

"LUCY! I forgot!" Frog bounced so hard on Dad's lap that he fell off. Picking himself up without comment, he kept bouncing. "Will she stay with us? Can I stay in a tent with her?"

Papa went to get his big yellow rain slicker, which made him look, Jax thought, like Big Bird. "Lucy's staying at the Inn until we take off next week," he said. "She and Elon want a little more privacy than an air mattress in our living room. He's psyched to finally see the island, after hearing about it for so long." Papa laughed a little and gave Jax a wink. "Elon on Rock Island . . . this is going to be good."

As they slowly wound along the rain-covered road toward town, Jax's mind was racing. He stared out the window at the wind-churned dune grass and, in the distance, the ocean's whitecaps. They had almost reached town when a huge white SUV careened around a curve, taking it way too fast, and nearly ran into them.

Papa swore and swerved to the side, narrowly missing the wooden fence and lurching hard into a low ditch.

"What kind of a—" Papa ranted, swearing loudly and repeatedly while peering over his shoulder.

The white car, already just a blur in the distance, soon disappeared.

"What kind of a fool driver is that? He's bound to kill himself! Are you boys all okay? You, Froggie?" Dad asked, turning around to make sure they were fine.

Jax nodded, but his heart was beating crazy-fast, like it did when he fell off his bike. It was scarier after it happened.

"That was Kark's car," Eli said quietly. "Big surprise."

Papa snorted. "That man. He needs to get OFF this island."

Jax couldn't have agreed more. He thought about

Elon, and about how he always said the secret to his trick was deflection—getting people to look at his left hand while his right hand was reaching into their pocket, or behind their ear.

"Dad, Papa," he said, leaning forward in the car as Papa maneuvered the van back onto the road, cursing under his breath. "I have to ask you something. I know you don't want us spying anymore—"

Dad started to break in, but Jax spoke over him. "—and I won't. But I'm begging you! Can't you guys look into this dude? Something is seriously sketchy about him! And if he's somehow messing with our lighthouse . . ." He trailed off.

Dad looked at Papa. "We can do some basic asking around, I suppose," he said slowly. "What exactly do you think he's doing, Jax?"

Frog spoke up. "I heard him! He wants to sell containers for millions of dollars! And he said it's in the bag!"

Dad and Papa exchanged bemused looks. "We'll take a look," Papa said finally. "But remember, boys, this is likely not going to yield much. He's a fool and a terrible driver—"

"—and he wears awful shorts. Just . . . there's no excuse for those shorts," Dad interrupted.

"—but that's not criminal behavior. Chances are we aren't going to find much of interest," Papa finished. "And assuming we don't, you need to let this go." His voice softened.

"Look. I know this is hard. It's hard for us too. I've been watching that lighthouse from my bedroom window for as long as I can remember. It's been a constant part of our lives." He sighed. "But things do change, whether we want them to or not. And some changes are good, while others might break our hearts a bit. But either way, remember the wise words of the wonderful Theodor Geisel, otherwise known as Dr. Seuss."

"I know him!" Frog interrupted.

"He said, 'Don't cry because it's over, smile because it happened,' " Papa went on. "And that might be a pretty good way to think about our time with the Rock Island lighthouse."

The car fell silent as Papa drove on along the twisty turns of the shore road, windshield wipers pushing against the driving rain.

Chapter Twenty

IN WHICH LUCY LISTENS TO IT ALL

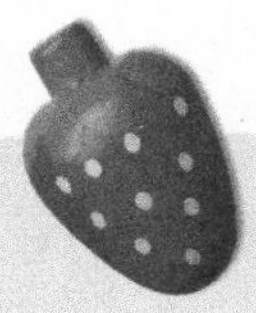

August 28

Hey, Luce,

Come on over as soon as you wake up. As you've probably gathered by now, everyone is in pieces. Sam hates his costume; Eli and Jax are brokenhearted over the lighthouse; Jax has something else going on, but we'll get into that later; and Frog is mad because none of us knows quite what to do with the information that "Kark wants to make containers and sell them for millions." I'm sorry Elon has to wander into this madhouse. Though as I remember, he always says, "Not my zebra. Not my zoo." A fine philosophy ...

Jason

At least the sun had come out, Eli thought. If he'd had to stay cooped up in the house for one more day with his whole grouchy family he would have lost his mind. Lucy and Elon had helped, of course, coming over and playing games and, in Elon's case, doing some excellent magic tricks. But the Nugget was a small house. And when six Fletchers, Lucy, Elon, Sir Puggleton, Zeus, and Lili were all inside, it felt like an explosion waiting to happen. It didn't help that every time Elon laughed his big, deep laugh, Sir Puggleton would start barking wildly. Eli was ready for a break.

Finally the sun came out, and after a perfect day of waves at the big beach, he and Jax had brought Lucy and Elon to the cove for an afternoon paddle. Jax and Elon had started paddling toward the far rocks while Eli and Lucy pulled farther ahead, the late-afternoon light turning the water into a glorious, glittering web.

"I am *impressed*!" Lucy said, shaking her head in pretend disbelief. "Your papa said you had nailed this, but I admit, I was prepared to take extraordinary measures and tow us both in to shore. Instead, you're schooling me! Whoa!" In her excitement, Lucy swung her arms up and the boat lurched to the side.

"Careful!" Eli called, laughing at the expression on her face. "Yeah. Once I fell out of the boat, it really made a difference."

They paddled in companionable silence for a while, enjoying the sun and the water. Then Lucy spoke up.

"So what's been going on this summer? I mean, other than the terrible lighthouse stuff. Someone's finally back in the big captain's house, huh?"

Eli nodded. "Yeah. The Galindos. But we don't know where they are! They've been gone for a few days, and we don't have their phone number or anything. It's weird. Anyway, they're pretty awesome, though at first we thought . . . well, we thought Val, the older one, was a total pain. She had a friend visiting . . . this totally annoying girl. And the two of them were all 'Sam's so cute! Boys!' until I thought Sam would punch them. But once Janie left, Val actually turned out to be pretty cool. She wants to make movies—well, she's the one who made the video of Lili swimming!"

"I loved that! She's pretty talented," Lucy interrupted.

"Yeah. So anyway, the *other* Galindo kid—that would be Alex—is cool. A lot like Jax, always messing around with snakes and crabs and stuff, or wanting to play sports. But here's the thing: she has really short hair, and always wears huge old T-shirts and stuff. She even wears board shorts and swim shirts at the beach. And her name is Alex! Well, actually, it's Alexandra, but we never knew that. So . . ."

"So . . . what? You thought she was a boy? No! Was that totally embarrassing?" Lucy asked, forgetting to paddle.

"Kind of. We were at a fancy brunch and she came

in wearing a dress. Jax nearly died." Eli laughed at the memory.

"Anyway, they've been really fun. Especially since Sam's been . . . well, he's busy, you know. With the play and all." Eli fell silent. He didn't want to say that this summer, while pretty good, didn't feel like any of their old summers. The lack of the lighthouse, the Galindo girls, Sam always rushing off to rehearsal . . . it wasn't like it used to be.

As though reading his mind, Lucy spoke. "You know, you guys are so lucky to be a gang of four. There's always someone around to play with. I mean, when I was little and Jason went away to camp, that was it. I was bored senseless until he got home." She was silent a minute. "But even so, the older you boys get, the more you're going to each develop your own things. Your own interests, your own activities, your own friends. But that doesn't mean you won't have each other."

Eli nodded quickly. "I know," he said. "I know that."

Lucy smiled. "I know you know. You're a pretty smart dude. But what you might not know is that I think—my hypothesis, if you will—is that you guys will always have each other as touchstones, and places like this will bring you together, even if some of the details change over time." She looked over her shoulder at Eli, who had slowed. "Does that make sense? WHOA!" she cried as she wobbled again.

Eli laughed a little, then sighed. "Yeah. I just . . . want things to stay the same, I guess." He sighed again. "I was so sure we could save the lighthouse. I had it all worked out that we could do a bunch of fund-raisers and get the whole town involved and make a ton of money. But . . . I don't know. We all got kind of fed up. Or discouraged. Or . . . just distracted, I guess."

Lucy looked back at him. "You know you can't blame yourself for this, right?" she asked. "I'm not saying it wasn't a good idea. But putting the pressure on yourself and your brothers to raise a half a million dollars . . . that's not fair."

Eli nodded. "I know." He *did* know, but it felt good to hear Lucy say it. A tiny worried part of him loosened, just a little bit.

He looked up toward the horizon, where the sun was getting low. "We should turn back. I wonder how far Elon and Jax went," he said, expertly paddling the kayak in a wide circle.

Lucy followed. "Probably nothing too ambitious. Elon wasn't too sure about this whole kayak thing. . . . He's never been in one. Still, the man can balance on the edge of a wall, pull champagne bottles out of thin air, and disappear from a room. I'm pretty sure he can handle a kayak."

When they got back to shore, Elon and Jax were already there. After pulling their kayaks up on the rocks, Lucy and Eli joined them.

“How’d you do?” Lucy asked, shoving Elon over on the beach towel. “Jax show you how it’s done?”

Elon laughed his big deep laugh. “Oh, I did fine. I just . . . that’s a teeny-tiny boat! I’m a big tall man! I felt like some kind of Weeble-wobble toy out there!”

Jax giggled. “You should have seen it!” he said to Eli. “He got in and the boat, like, sank. I mean, not all the way, obviously, but down pretty far. And Elon . . .” Jax laughed harder and Elon punched him. “He just had this look on his face, like ‘Whose idea was this?’ He looked like Zeus whenever he’s stuck on top of a cabinet or something.”

Elon gave Jax a look over the top of his sunglasses. “Oh, that’s right. Mock me. Mock *me,* the Great Elon!” He waved a hand like he was disgusted, but Jax just laughed harder.

Lucy kissed Elon’s cheek. “Poor baby.”

Jax lay back flat on his towel, staring toward the rocks.

Eli leaned over.

“So . . . did Dad hear anything back from Natalia or John? It’s kind of weird that they’re just *gone.*”

Jax shook his head. “He said there was no answer at the house. He doesn’t have their cell phone numbers, since they never work around here anyway.”

“Where do you think they could be? Do you think something’s wrong?” Eli pressed.

Jax just shrugged. “Who knows? But Sam’s dress

rehearsal is tomorrow, and if he doesn't talk to Val before then he's going to bust a gasket. He's freaking out."

"Have you guys seen any of the play?" Lucy asked. "What do you think?"

"We watched part of a rehearsal. It's pretty good," Eli said.

"I don't like the way they talk . . . all the *thee*s and *thou*s make it hard to figure out what's going on," Jax complained.

Lucy nodded. "Yeah, I can see that. But it's a pretty funny story. All these crazy fairies messing around with us mortals, playing games and using magic spells just to screw stuff up."

"Yeah! They make these two guys totally crazy for this one girl, and everyone's freaking out and running around in the woods. But the best part is when that dumb guy gets turned into an ass!" Eli said.

Jax snickered.

"Ass meaning donkey, dum-dum," Eli said, but Jax just kept laughing.

Elon joined him. "It would be kind of funny, if he turned into a big old butt," he murmured, and Lucy swatted him.

"Thanks for keeping the toilet humor going," she said, before turning back to Eli.

"I think my favorite line of that play—and it's so cool, because Sam gets to say it—is 'What fools these mortals be!' That's us. We're the foolish mortals, running around panicking over blond wigs and friends who wear dresses occasionally"—Jax looked up sharply, and, grinning, Lucy went on—"and even the lighthouse! Our wonderful lighthouse! Well, we foolish mortals think we're in charge, but changes happen. And sometimes good stuff comes out of them."

Eli looked skeptical. "I don't see what's so good about losing the lighthouse," he said. "I think it stinks. It will never be the same here. Never."

Lucy nodded. "True. But sometimes not being the same can be even better."

Chapter Twenty-One

IN WHICH SAM REALIZES THE SHOW MUST GO ON (BUT SORT OF WISHES IT DIDN'T)

CAPTAIN JIM'S ISLAND NEWS
August 29, 8:00 a.m.

Well, folks, the summer is winding down, but before you pack your bags, wash out the lobster pot one last time, and board the ferry, make sure you get your tickets to the Actors' Project production of *A Midsummer Night's Dream.* It's written by some English guy named Billy, but I hear it's pretty funny. See you there.

Meanwhile, some of you may have heard about a certain cat swimming about in the lovely seas of Rock Island. Yes, the rumor is true. . . . Lili the kitten, who belongs to the Fletcher family, is the star of a new Internet video. You can find a link to it on the Rock Island Chamber of Commerce website. Come on in, the water's fine!

It was the worst rehearsal Sam had ever been to. He stood backstage, listening to Alan yelling at the four actors who played the lovers.

"Come ON, people! We are live tomorrow! This is NOT the time to forget your blocking and bump into each other!"

The actors mumbled and shifted around onstage. Earlier they had botched an important scene where they needed to dash around searching for each other, and the play had ground to a stop.

"Okay, take it from the beginning of act four, scene one. And please focus. We don't have all day to get this right." Alan disappeared again, and the actors took their places.

Sam wiped his sweaty hands on his velvet knickers. He would come onstage shortly, watching the fairy queen, Titania, fall in love with the country fool, Bottom, whose head had turned into that of a donkey's. He wished he felt more in character. He couldn't stop worrying about the costume, panicking that Val had disappeared without ever coming up with whatever good idea she'd had to show Alan, assuming Alan even remembered. He couldn't go on in these knickers. And Alan had been so mad about the wig! Though he supposed he owed Zeus for at least getting rid of—

"SAM!" Alan's voice bellowed from the front of the house.

He had missed his cue.

His face hot and sweaty, Sam rushed onstage. "Sorry! Sorry." He took his position.

Alan looked disgusted, and Sam closed his eyes briefly, trying to remember the magic of learning to play a character, *becoming* that character for a little while, at least. He tried to remember who Puck was, a mischievous immortal who didn't really care about anything or anyone. He began to speak his first line.

From backstage, his phone rang, with a loud, embarrassing rap song that he'd programmed in as a joke. He froze.

"WHOSE PHONE IS THAT?" Alan screamed, now completely enraged.

Sam closed his eyes again, wishing more than anything in the world that he had never agreed to do this stupid play. "Sorry," he said again, and waited for the explosion.

But Alan just stood there for a minute, looking pained. Onstage, Teddy and Julia watched sympathetically. Julia winked once, trying to make Sam smile, but he couldn't manage it.

"Okay. Okay, it's fine. Terrible rehearsals can equal great performances. I've seen it happen. We just have to get through this." Alan seemed to be talking to himself, pacing and muttering.

Onstage the actors stood silently.

"Let's take a break. Sam, can I talk to you for a minute?" Alan said finally.

Sam sighed and slowly walked offstage.

When Sam got home from rehearsal he wanted nothing more than to disappear into his room and slam the door behind him. The only problem? He didn't have a room, or a door. Instead he had a tiny house filled with his three brothers, his aunt Lucy and her boyfriend, Elon, and both his parents, all loudly making dinner, setting the table, playing Monopoly, teasing the cat, and—it looked like—plotting world domination.

Sam scowled and walked straight through the house and out to the back deck. He stared at the landscape in front of him, the early-evening light turning everything a dim, glowing blue, the scrubby grass blowing and waving in the wind, and beyond, the lighthouse, looming as tall as ever behind its metal fence.

He sighed, feeling almost like crying. What the heck was wrong with him? It was just the end of summer, that was all. Just the changing of the seasons.

"What's on your mind?" Lucy asked from behind him.

Sam didn't turn around. He shrugged. "Nothing. Just thinking."

"About the lighthouse." It wasn't a question.

Sam shrugged again. "I guess. And the play. And stuff."

Lucy sat down on the edge of the deck, pulling Sam next to her. Sam sat with a thump, the warm wood feeling good in the quickly cooling evening air. It felt almost like fall. He lay back, staring up at the sky, and Lucy lay next to him.

"How was rehearsal?" she asked.

Sam gave a short laugh. "Well, it was brutal. Mostly. I kept screwing up, and so did a bunch of other people. But by the end we had kind of gotten it together. I mean, sort of."

"Are you nervous about tomorrow night?" she asked. "Shakespeare's a big change from *Annie*. But I suspect you're going to be great. There's so much fun and mischief and energy in that play, and you've got that to spare!"

"I'm not too nervous, but my costume is horrible. After today's rehearsal I wasn't about to even bring it up with Alan. But I guess I just have to deal with it. It's only for three performances." He sighed. "It's just weird, that's all. I mean, this summer . . . everything's different."

"What do you mean?" Lucy asked.

Sam's thoughts burst out like a dam breaking. "Well, let's see. This time last year we had the lighthouse. And I had never even thought about being in a play, let alone spending half my time in rehearsals. And now we hang out a ton with Val and Alex, and last year we didn't even know them, and this year it seems like all we're talking about is this stupid Kark guy, when before we didn't even know he existed. Nothing's the same!"

Lucy nodded slowly. "Yeah, I hear you. That is a lot of changes. Especially because . . . well, these things are taking up a huge part of your brain! I mean, the play alone is a big deal. Then add everything else!" She sighed and suddenly pointed. "Hey! Check it out. First star."

Sam looked. As he watched, more stars popped out, faint in the last light of the day.

"There's a lot that's changed this summer, that's for sure," Lucy went on. "But having been coming here since way before you were born, I can tell you that there's a lot that stays the same too. I mean, I used to lie here looking at the stars with your papa, talking about Archie comics and *The Brady Bunch,* and complaining that Mimi never let me bake anything in the kitchen because she said it got too hot." She turned to look at Sam again, and grinned. "I sure showed her, huh?"

Sam smiled too. He liked hearing about how long his family had been coming here. It made him feel more connected somehow. Less like things were slipping away from him.

"Anyway," Lucy went on, "I grew up here, had my first kiss here—don't worry, I'm not going to tell you about it! And I got my first summer job here, and even got my own place here, when I couldn't stand living with your grandparents anymore. And each summer, during those years, seemed totally different than the one before it. Except for the parts that stayed the same, you know?" She paused, and Sam shrugged.

"I guess," he said.

"Well, what's stayed the same for you this summer?" Lucy asked.

"Soccer in the yard. The beach. Riding the waves. Catching crabs at the cove. Gilly's fried clams," Sam said, after thinking for a minute.

"Right! And the chowder at the Sisterhood. And Captain Jim—he's been here forever," Lucy added.

"And second-mortgage muffins," Sam said. He propped himself up on his elbows and looked over the lawn. It was almost completely dark now, and, right on schedule, the beam of the lighthouse cut through the twilight.

Lucy laughed. "Yep. You know, I worked there one summer, washing dishes. I washed *thousands* of muffin tins. . . . I couldn't eat those muffins for a few years after that."

Sam laughed too. He was starting to feel better. They sat in silence for a minute, staring at the lighthouse beam as it swung around and around.

Papa walked out and joined them. "What's happening, Booger? How was rehearsal, Sammy?" he asked, sitting down next to them with a groan. "Whoa. The old bones are protesting."

"We're just talking about the whole time-flying thing," Lucy said. "I was remembering being out here—of course, the deck wasn't built, so we would just lie on the grass—when we were around Sam's age."

Papa nodded. "That's right. We would bring a blanket out and watch for shooting stars." He fell silent for a minute. "Man, that was a long time ago. How'd you get so old?"

Lucy reached across Sam to shove Papa, who tickled her, knocking Sam over in the process. Dad came out as they were all laughing and Papa was groaning in fake agony.

"Well, that's a sight I love to see. My favorite sister-in-law maiming her brother in a tickle battle," he said. "What a gorgeous night. We should have a campfire. There aren't too many nights left."

"That's what we were talking about, sort of," Lucy said, scooting over so that Dad could sit. "How time is flying by."

"*Tempus fugit* indeed," Dad said. He pulled Sam close to him in a tight one-armed hug. "This boy is sprouting in front of our eyes. As Cicero so wisely said—" he began, but Sam cut him off.

"No Latin speeches! Please!" Sam begged. It was bad enough when his parents got sentimental in English.

Dad laughed. "Fine. I'll save it for your high school graduation."

Sam smiled. "I can wait," he said. "No rush."

The night darkened around them, and as Sam looked up, star after star emerged, until the sky was littered with them and the Milky Way was fully visible. He remembered

Eli spouting on about astronomy: *The stars are always there, of course. We just can't always see them. Our circumstances change, not the stars.* Maybe there were a lot of things that stayed the same this year. Maybe they were all still there, just invisible.

Chapter Twenty-Two

IN WHICH IT'S SHOWTIME— FOR SAM AND LILI

August 30: www.funthings.com Check out the new Internet sensation, Lili the swimming cat! One million views of this hilarious and adorable kitten swimming in the refreshing waters off a tiny island in New England.

Frog felt like his world was exploding. The house was full to bursting, Sam was getting ready for opening night, Lucy, Elon, Dad, and Papa were in muttered conversations and had no time to talk about anything else, and they had only a few days left on the island. Frog was forlornly kicking a ball around the yard when suddenly Alex and Val ran over, panting and out of breath.

Frog ran toward them in amazement.

"Where have you been? We were worried! And Sam is mad about his costume! And our aunt Lucy is here! And—" he started.

Val cut him off. "I have to show you guys something! Where are your parents?"

Alex explained as they went to the house. "We went off-island for a funeral. Mami's *abuela* died suddenly. We came back with the babysitter so we could see Sam's play, but our parents won't be back until next week."

The three of them ran into the house. "Jason! Tom! I need to show you something! Come quick!" Val shouted, not even saying hello to Jax or Eli, who were on the floor sorting shells.

Frog followed Val, wondering what had gotten into her. She was talking to his parents like a grown-up, he thought. It must be important.

Papa came out from his office, with Dad, Lucy, and Elon trailing behind. "Valerie! You're back! What's going on with you guys?"

"Funeral. Mami's *abuela*. Texas." Alex spoke in fast bullet points. "But that's not important right now. Check out what Val has!"

They crowded around Val, introducing Lucy and Elon and trying to talk over one another as they looked at what she was holding. It was her head-mounted video camera, the one she had loaned Frog that day at the cove.

"I didn't realize Frog had turned this thing on," Val started. "I thought the battery was dead from the beginning. But it seems he turned it on in the car and just let it run until the battery died. So it was filming the whole time."

Frog jumped up and down. "Did it get Lili swimming toward me? Is it as good as your video? Did you know your video is on the town website? Dad showed me. We're famous!"

Val interrupted him. "It's better than that. Remember you were trying to tell me that you heard Kark on the phone? Listen to this!" She pressed Play and they all strained to hear.

"Hah! No, I was only kidding. It's worth it, even with all the provincial yahoos. We're ninety percent there. The inspectors are on the site as we speak, and I have them buttoned up."

Pause.

"Not to worry. They're airtight. They're not even taking real estimates. . . . They'll go with whatever I give them. It's in the bag."

There was silence in which they could only hear Frog's breathing, fast and nervous. Then Kark again.

"This time next year there will be gorgeous condominiums where that broken-down piece of rock is! And once they're up I don't ever need to come back here. So hang in there . . . we've almost got it. And believe me, with the kind of restrictions they have on building here, we can easily charge three to four million apiece. Easily! Everyone wants in on this place, because it's so 'unspoiled'! By Labor Day at the latest. I'll keep in touch."

The voice faded away, and the sounds of splashing grew louder and louder. Val turned the video off.

"See?" she said, looking around her at their shocked faces. "He *is* totally crooked!"

They all stood silently for a second, trying to digest this. Then Frog stomped his foot.

"I TOLD YOU!" he bellowed. "I TOLD YOU SO!"

Everyone started talking at once.

The grown-ups were in a frenzy. There seemed to be a lot of talk about what to do first: if they should go to the police station, or if they needed to contact town hall.

Papa swore. "We need to get to the theater! The show is going to start in less than an hour. We don't have time to deal with this. Besides, no one's going to be in their offices at this hour."

At this, Val gave a little scream. "*¡Ay!* And Sam's costume! Mami and I worked on something awesome and then I wasn't even here to give it to him! Is it too late? What's he wearing?"

"The totally lame girlie outfit that's insanely bad and he's freaking out," Jax said. Then he looked guilty. "Sorry. I mean . . . it's just kind of dumb."

Val chewed on her lip. "I need to get a ride to town. NOW. He's going to love the costume we designed, and Alan really liked it when I told him about it before we left." She looked near tears. "*¡Maldición!*"

Papa looked up from where he was scrolling through

the video. "We'll drive you in if you can leave now. Right, Tom? We told Sam we'd stop by early to wish him luck. Then we can try to find some of the town councilors, though as I said, I doubt they'll be available."

Dad looked a little panicked. He ran his hands through his hair, which stood up wildly. "Lucy, can you and Elon bring the rest of the gang before curtain? You can't be late! Deal?"

Lucy nodded and promised that she'd get them there on time.

Papa grabbed the keys. "Okay, Val, if you're ready to go, we'll leave now. Not sure if the director will be too keen on a late costume change, but it's worth a try! Ready?"

Val looked down at herself. She was less fancy than usual, Frog noticed, wearing plain old shorts and a pink T-shirt. He frowned. He liked Val's more exciting outfits. But Val just gave a little sigh and nodded.

"Yeah. It doesn't matter what I look like. Not when we have a chance to save Sam from velvet knickers! Let's go!"

They rushed out the door, shouting dire warnings about the need to upload the video somewhere and save it. The screen door slammed behind them, and then it was silent.

The rest of the group looked at each other.

"Well," Frog said, a little testily. He was still mad no one believed him, and no one was going to say how clever he was for getting the video! After all, he *had* gotten it, even if he didn't know it. He should get some credit.

"We need a plan!" Eli said.

"Yeah! And fast!" Jax scratched a mosquito bite. "How does a citizen's arrest work in real life?"

Lucy put her hands up, calling a halt. "Let's think this through before doing anything too crazy."

Elon looked indignant. "What makes you think we're going to do something crazy? Just because this creep is engaged in major criminal deception involving the bribery of a corporate entity, not to mention breaking the hearts of some of my favorite people, what crazy thing would we do?"

"Punch him in the nose?" Frog offered.

"Put him in the stocks in the town square!" Eli added. He was reading *Johnny Tremain* and kept talking about the Revolutionary War.

"Poop on him!" Frog screamed, overcome.

Alex fell to the floor laughing. "Poop! On him!" she repeated, rolling around.

"Gentlemen! Oh, and lady," Lucy added. "Calm down. We need to get ready for Sam's play; we can figure out the video after. Right, Elon?"

"But what if he leaves?" Frog said, his voice squeaky with panic. "He said 'Labor Day at the latest'! And that's soon, right?"

"It's the day after we leave," Eli said. "Only a few days away!"

"Don't worry, guys. We have the video, and he's not going to disappear," Lucy said.

"But I want to *see* him squirm! I want him to get *owned*. Right here on the island," Alex said. Jax and Eli nodded.

Lucy was about to answer when Lili flew into the room, chasing a fly. She gave a low caterwaul, then launched herself at the wall, hitting it above Frog's head, before pushing off and bounding into the kitchen. They all stopped and stared at the cat as she tore around the house.

"That cat's insane," Alex said. "I've never seen anything like it."

The sounds of mad scuffling came from the kitchen, and Zeus ran out with Lili in fast pursuit.

Lucy looked dazed. "I'll say," she answered, shaking her head.

Jax looked over at Alex. "Hey! Did you know that video Val made of Lili has gone totally viral! It's all over the Internet. . . . There have been, like, a million views."

"I wonder if there's more on *my* video," Frog said, still feeling proud he had turned on the camera, even though he hadn't known it. "Maybe Val can make another one."

Elon stared at him. "What did you say, big man?" he asked, his eyes fixed on Frog.

Frog felt important. "Maybe Val can make another video of Lili from *my* camera. I mean, the one from the camera on my head. The one that has the bad Kark stuff," he clarified, because Elon was still staring at him.

Then Elon started to laugh. It began as a kind of quiet chuckle, but then turned into a full-blown HAHAHA-HAHA that had Jax and Eli laughing too, even though nobody knew what was so funny. Sir Puggleton started to bark.

"THAT'S IT!" Elon bellowed finally. "The YouTube channel! It's gotten a million hits, and there's a link to it from the Rock Island Chamber of Commerce. We can upload the video of Kark's conversation there, and let the public see for themselves!"

Lucy smiled slowly, then burst out laughing. "Well, that's a thought. What's the worst that can happen? It's pretty clear-cut. . . . Thank goodness this island has such terrible phone reception. The man was practically screaming. I say we do it." She looked at Elon's watch. "But we have to hurry. We can't be late for the play."

The two of them rushed into the office with the camera.

In the living room, Jax, Eli, Alex, and Frog looked at each other.

Frog scowled. He still hadn't gotten any praise for his video, and none of his stupid brothers had even said he was right. It had sounded like Kark said *containers*. So what if it had actually been *condiments* or whatever?

Jax walked over and solemnly held out his hand. "Frog Fletcher, you were right. You did hear that trash-head say he was going to make millions tearing down the lighthouse. I give you full credit as the best detective the Fletcher family has."

Frog beamed. "I know," he said, and shook his brother's hand, hard.

Chapter Twenty-Three

IN WHICH THE FLETCHERS (AND ELON) BRING DOWN THE HOUSE

Sam, hopefully someone gives this to you backstage. We found Alan and he says it's fine (though he didn't look particularly like he even heard us). But anyway, he said okay, so here it is. Don't wear the knickers! Repeat: DON'T WEAR THE KNICKERS!!

Break a leg, Val

Eli loved *A Midsummer Night's Dream*. It was way better than the rehearsal, and frankly way better than it had sounded when Sam tried to explain it. After all, Sam kept going on about lovers and fairy queens and stuff that sounded bizarre for a play, and even more bizarre for Sam to care about. But somehow the story—and especially Sam's totally wild and funny Puck—was way better than

Eli had expected. He managed to forget about Kark and the lighthouse and the video for a little while, as the characters were bewitched, fought over stupid things, and, best of all, got messed with by Sam, who crept among them like a weird, grinning imp, squeezing magic potion in their eyes to make them fall in love with the wrong people. Eli noted with relief that Sam was *not* wearing a wig or a pair of velvet knickers. Instead he was painted a pale bluish white and wore raggedy green silk pants and a dark undershirt-type thing. He looked strong and dangerous and strange . . . a good look, Eli thought, for the totally troublemaking Puck. His master, the fairy king Oberon, also looked cool. He was played by a guy with a beard and sand-colored dreadlocks who Eli knew was a lifeguard on Surf Beach. He loomed over everyone, tall and disdainful-looking, as Sam bounced and jumped and ran around him like some wild pet.

It was intermission before Eli knew it, and he blinked in the sudden brightness of the theater lights. All around him people were standing up, chattering and laughing. In front of him, Alex and Val turned around and pointed.

"There he is! Look!" Alex whisper-shouted. She pointed toward the stage, where, sure enough, Chase Kark and his terrible green shorts were standing.

"We need to tell people! We need to—" Val started, but Alex pulled her back.

"We took care of it. Trust us." She turned to the

Fletchers and Elon. “Let’s go out to the lobby. And bring your phone,” she added to Lucy, winking.

Lucy winked back and they began to push through the crowd.

“Wasn’t Sam terrific?” Dad asked, when he had caught up to Eli, Jax, and Frog. “What did you guys think of your brother?”

“He was sick,” Jax said. “Totally cool. But what’s with those stupid ‘youths of Athens,’ or whatever? They’re seriously weak. Especially that Demetrius guy. What a loser.”

“He’s not a loser. He’s been magicked. It happens,” Eli said, but Jax just shrugged. “Whatever. They’re all nuts. When’s the guy getting turned into a donkey? I can’t wait for that part!”

They made it to the lobby, which was crowded with Rock Island regulars, from Captain Jim to Officer Levee. It was hot and loud, with, Eli thought, far too many people kissing and hugging and yelling hellos. The island was only ten miles long! How much time could it have possibly been since they had all seen each other last? Dad and Papa disappeared into the throng.

Eli grimaced as Jax accidentally stepped on his foot.

“Sorry. I’m trying to see if we can find any of the town council people,” Jax said, standing on tiptoe and trying to look over Eli’s head.

Eli, who was still several inches taller, looked over

Jax and into the crowd. "I don't see any— Wait! There's Kark!" He punched Jax to get his attention. "Right near Dad and Papa and Frog! Come on, let's go!"

Grabbing Alex and Val, who were trying to convince their babysitter to get them lemonade and homemade chocolate chip cookies from the concession stand, they headed off through the crowded lobby. On the far side of the room, Lucy, Elon, Dad, and Papa were talking to a bunch of other grown-ups, right next to Kark, who was on his phone.

"Dad!" Jax called as they got closer.

"Papa!" Eli said at the same time.

"Jason, we really need to—" Alex started.

Papa and Dad both held up their hands. "Whoa! Let's try again, this time with manners," Dad said. "Alex and Val, it's great to see you both. Val, your costume idea for Sam's Puck was perfect! He looks terrific. Way better than that knickers thing he had going on. He owes you."

Val waved him off impatiently. "Thanks, but not now! We need to show—"

Dad spoke over her. "Hold up there, Val. We were just introducing Elon. Elon Reynolds, Carol Chittenden and Bruce Colvin."

The grown-ups shook hands and said how-do-you-do type things. Carol asked Elon where he was from, and before long Elon was talking about his career as a magician, traveling around on giant cruise ships and to clubs in Las Vegas. Usually Eli loved hearing Elon talk about his job. After all, how many magicians did you get to meet in your life? And Elon was always doing fun things like taking someone's watch right off their wrist or their belt off their pants without them knowing. But today Eli could only look at Kark's terrible green shorts and worry about what was going to happen next. To his horror he saw that, next to his stupid tan legs in their green shorts, Kark had a suitcase on wheels that he was keeping very close. Maybe Frog was right! Maybe Kark was leaving the island! They couldn't let him get away.

Eli pushed himself into the middle of the grown-ups. "We have to show you something!" he shouted, trying to be heard over their chatter.

He felt a hand on his head, heavy and reassuring. Looking up he saw Elon smiling down at him. Elon winked.

"The kids made another great video," he said, his deep voice full of hidden laughter. "And I . . . errm . . . took the liberty of getting it ready for you." He grinned.

"Check your phone," Elon said to Carol.

Carol reached down to unsnap her straw purse. She peered inside. "It's not here!" she cried in surprise.

"That's odd," Elon said, but he was grinning even wider. "Bruce, why don't you check your back pocket?"

Looking startled, Bruce reached behind him and, with a laugh, pulled out a bright pink flowered phone case. "Well, this isn't mine," he said, handing it to Carol.

"How on earth?" Carol asked, staring at Elon. "I don't remember you moving this whole time! How did you get behind Bruce?"

Elon laughed and held his hands up, the picture of innocence. "The illusion is always about keeping the attention off where the real action is happening," he said, rocking back on his heels.

Eli noticed Elon rocking closer to Kark and the suitcase. He squinted at Elon. What did he have in mind?

Dad and Papa laughed, but Lucy punched Elon on the arm. "You can't steal Carol's phone! I used to babysit for her kids! There has got to be some rule about family friends!"

Carol shook her head, smiling. "Nonsense! That was the best trick I've ever seen."

Elon smiled. "Oh, there's all kinds of tricks," he said. "Now, you should check out that video. Those Fletcher kids are really something."

Carol turned on her phone and burst out laughing. "You seem to have the video all cued up! I guess I shouldn't ask how you did that," she said, shaking her head again. "You are one tricky man, Mr. Reynolds."

Elon smiled his sleepy smile and pretended to take a hat off his head, making a long, low bow and stretching his arms out wide. "I try, Ms. Chittenden," he said. "I try."

Carol pressed Play, and soon the sound of splashing

water and the occasional cawing gull came through. Then, loud and clear, came Kark's voice.

Eli closed his eyes and listened.

"What—" Carol began, but Bruce shushed her.

Next to them, Kark stiffened and froze in place.

Elon's smile grew.

"I—I don't understand," Bruce stammered. "What . . . ? How . . . ? Where . . . ?"

Dad looked like he had been hit by a two-by-four. "Boys?" he asked.

"It doesn't matter where it came from! What matters is that this . . . this . . . ," Carol sputtered.

"Officer Levee! Officer Maws! Can you come over here please!" Bruce called across the lobby. The two officers came strolling over.

Eli watched as Kark made a sudden dash for the door. But he didn't get far.

"AAAARRRGGH!" He bellowed, falling forward on his face.

Chase Kark was not a small man, nor a graceful one. He fell like a tree. Carol, Bruce, Dad, Papa, and Lucy sprang out of the way as he dropped, but Elon stayed in place, one hand casually on Kark's suitcase.

"What? WHO DID THIS?" Kark yelled.

Eli looked down at him and burst out laughing. Kark's shoelaces had been looped together and through the wheels of his suitcase. He wasn't going anywhere.

"This is outrageous! To think that this . . . this . . . this OFF-ISLANDER thought that he could tear down our lighthouse and build condominiums! Why, there will be a full criminal inquiry, starting Monday!" Bruce bellowed.

"Monday is the Labor Day picnic," Carol said distractedly, "and you're in charge of the lobster races. But Tuesday . . . Tuesday we will begin legal proceedings against him!"

"And add a citizen's arrest for his terrible shorts," Dad added.

Lucy burst out laughing.

"I still don't understand—" Bruce began. But just then the lights in the lobby began flashing on and off.

"Oh! The second act of the play is starting!" Papa said. "I almost forgot we were in the middle of *A Midsummer Night's Dream*. Seems like we're in the middle of a late-summer night's mystery! Someday, hopefully, someone can explain what just happened there," he added as they walked back to their seats.

"But what about him?" Jax asked, pointing at Kark, who was struggling, red-faced and livid, to undo his shoelaces. Apparently Elon had made some very tricky knots.

"Mr. Kark, you can wait out here with me," Officer Levee said. She wasn't smiling, but Eli got the feeling that she was plenty happy. "We can talk, if you'd like. But I should, of course, remind you: you have the right to remain silent. You have the right to an attorney . . ." Her voice drifted away as Eli walked back into the theater. It was time to watch the rest of the play.

The play got better and better. The country bumpkin actors were ridiculous, and the one who got turned into a donkey was the funniest of all, strutting around like a rock star and making Elon laugh so hard that the people in the row ahead of them told him to quiet down.

Finally, with Puck's help, all the humans found themselves in love with the right person, and the dumb donkey-headed guy was normal again, and everyone was happy. Then Sam stood onstage, staring out at them, otherworldly and awesome with his face paint and tattered costume. He spoke.

> *"If we shadows have offended,*
> *Think but this, and all is mended,*
> *That you have but slumber'd here,*
> *While these visions did appear.*
> *And this weak and idle theme,*
> *No more yielding but a dream,*
> *Gentles, do not reprehend:*
> *If you pardon, we will mend."*

The theater was totally silent. Then, with no warning, Sam leapt up onto a rope and was gone, leaving the empty stage behind.

* * *

That night, once the Fletchers had hugged Lucy and Elon goodnight and promised Val and Alex that they would see them in the morning, once they had taken Sam out for his celebratory three-scoop chocolate-marshmallow-whipped-cream sundae, once they had driven the dark, winding shore road back to the Nugget, Eli lay in bed. Around him the slow breathing of his brothers rustled the silence. Frog gave an incomprehensible babble, then rolled over and fell back asleep.

But Eli was awake. The light from Rock Island lighthouse swung through the room, momentarily illuminating the sloping walls and pinned-up posters. Eli was too excited to sleep. Sure, they had to leave in two days. They would be leaving Anna the seal, and Captain Jim and Julia, who was staying on at the marine lab for a semester before returning to college. They would be leaving the kayaks and the satisfying dip and swoop of the paddles in the water. They would be leaving the Galindo girls, who had become an unforgettable part of the summer.

But Eli wasn't sad. They were going back to Shipton. Back to Teddy and Jamil and Shipton Upper Elementary, back to his own cozy bed with no sand in it and only Jax to share a room with. Back to emails with Anna Bean and a chance to work on his giant Lego model. He sighed and stretched, rolling over to try to look out the window. A fingernail moon hung in the sky, providing just enough light to see the lighthouse gleaming whitely against the sky. Eli remembered the play, and Sam's words. Parts of this summer *felt* like a dream, like some kind of crazy adventure that had happened to some other, wilder family. It had been exciting, that was for sure. But, he thought, as he let his body melt into the slightly sandy sheets, it would be good to get back to the way things used to be.

Chapter Twenty-Four

IN WHICH IT IS TIME TO LEAVE THE ISLAND

Jax

I wanted to get you a goodbye present, but the babysitter said that a live green snake is not a cool gift, which is totally untrue, but whatever. I'm really glad we finally got to Rock Island. . . . I'd been hearing about it for years but never really thought it would be so awesome. We are definitely coming next summer, and hopefully we can have water fights and sleepovers in the lighthouse. Until then, hasta luego, amigo. Check you later.

Alex (andra . . . a girl. Duh . . . did you really think I didn't know what you thought? BUTTER!)

Leaving Rock Island at the end of summer vacation was always awful. Even though Jax was psyched to see his friends at home, the packing, chasing down of lost soccer balls, mad cleaning, and general mayhem that was required to get six Fletchers out of the Nugget made a sad day even worse. Add the early-morning departure, and usually at least one boy was crying and another in a rage before they even got out of the driveway. But finally they were at the ferry dock with Lucy and Elon, almost ready to say their last goodbyes. They stood outside the car, waiting to unload the animals and carry-on bags.

Lucy clapped her hands and glanced at Elon. "Before anyone goes anywhere, there's something we need to tell you guys," she said, looping her arm through Elon's. "It's not completely finalized, but Elon and I are pretty sure it's going to work." She took a deep breath and paused.

Jax balanced on one foot, using the other to scratch a mosquito bite on his calf. Why was Lucy being so mysterious?

Finally she spoke again. "We're setting up a nonprofit to buy the lighthouse, fix it up, open all the closed-up rooms, and use it as an artists' retreat—real artists, not scams like that guy! Artists will be able to come and stay and make beautiful art on the island."

"Especially diverse artists. Got to get some more brothers on this rock," Elon added, laughing a little and shaking his head. "If this place were any whiter and richer, it'd be a cheesecake." He flashed Jax a thumbs-up while Papa groaned.

Jax almost dropped his second-mortgage muffin,

which he had grabbed from the bag Dad was holding. He stared at his aunt, then at his brothers. Then the Fletchers all started talking at once.

"Wait, you'd *own* it?"

"That's so cool!"

"But then we couldn't go in it!"

"That would mean it's still off-limits!"

Lucy held up her hands. "It would be an artists' retreat . . . *except* for the month of August. In August it would remain free and open to the public. Forever."

"Forever," Eli echoed.

"Forever and ever?" Frog asked.

"Well," Lucy said. "For as long as we can imagine."

The boys digested this for a moment. Then Jax whooped and high-fived Elon, and Eli hugged Lucy so hard she squeaked.

"You can have all the money we raised!" Eli said. "It's only a hundred and thirteen dollars, including my birthday money, but at least it's something, right?"

"It's everything," Lucy said, hugging him back. "Your plan gave me the idea in the first place. If it weren't for you, I wouldn't have been brave enough to try."

"What's going to happen to Kark?" Jax asked, still too shocked to finish chewing his bite of muffin.

Lucy shrugged, looking supremely unconcerned. "Who knows? Lawsuits, probably. Jail time, doubtfully, unfortunately. He's got enough money to slither out of it,

I bet. But who cares? One thing's for sure—he's not getting our lighthouse!"

"How did you pull this off? Dad? Papa? Did you know?" Sam asked, turning so fast from one parent to the other that he looked like Lili watching a fly.

"We had an idea, but they played it pretty close to the chest," Papa said, throwing an arm around Lucy and another around Elon. "Sneaky buggers, aren't they? Good thing they're on our side!"

Frog, caught up in the excitement, launched himself at Papa, trying to wrap his arm around all three of them. Jax joined in and grabbed hold; then Eli, Sam, and Dad followed suit, until they were a yelping, whooping knot trying to keep from falling over.

Jax didn't let go until the line of cars waiting to drive down into the ferry started to move. Dad untangled himself and quickly said goodbye to Lucy and Elon as the others frantically grabbed the cats and Sir Puggleton and everything else they needed. Then Dad moved the van into the line of cars. Soon Lucy and Elon were waving goodbye as the Fletchers stood in the long, winding line to board the ferry, signaling the official end to their Rock Island summer.

Even with the astonishing, amazing, mind-blowing good news, standing in line was brutal.

"EW! Lili totally gacked and it's coming out the front of the carrier!" Jax yelled. He put the wailing cat down and wiped his hands on Eli's shirt. Eli shrieked and jumped out of his way.

Sir Puggleton began to bark at a dog down the dock, and several people around them in the ferry line shifted toward the gangplank.

"Jax, can you please just . . . deal with it?" Papa asked. He was carrying an enormous cooler, Sir Puggleton's leash, and two tote bags full of fragile "specimens," as Eli called the shells and rocks he was bringing back.

"Why can't someone else take this stupid cat?" Jax complained. "I'll take Zeus."

"You can't even lift Zeus," Sam answered. He had Zeus's carrier in one hand, but his arm muscles were bulging from the effort. In his other, he had his phone, which was pinging with some terribly annoying bird noise that Val had set up as a goodbye gift.

"I have to go. Papa? PAPA! I have to GO," Frog said suddenly, appearing at Papa's elbow.

Papa gave a wild-eyed look around and thrust the tickets at Sam and Sir Puggleton's leash at Eli, who was already staggering with three bags of leftover groceries. "Go on up. I'll be back shortly!" He darted through the crowd with Frog close at his heels. Frog's bathroom visits often came with little warning.

Slowly the line moved forward, and finally Jax, Eli, and

Sam boarded the ferry. Before too long a very relieved-looking Papa appeared with Frog; then Dad came up from the car deck. They gathered on the top deck and looked out over the island.

"Is the loud horn going to sound now? Is it, Papa?" Frog asked, keeping an eye on the giant smokestack.

Papa dropped all his bags and lay on the bench with a sigh. "Not yet, Froggie. Soon, but not yet."

Jax stared at the island. It was early morning, but the dock was bustling. He could see Captain Jim's slip, already empty. Captain Jim must have set out early to fish. Farther away, he could make out the tip of the lighthouse. Although he couldn't see it, Jax knew that their house was right next to it, nestled up alongside, where it had always been.

Dad came up and squeezed him. "You okay, my sweet son?" he asked. "It's been quite a summer, don't you think? That's pretty amazing news about the lighthouse, hey?"

Jax nodded. It had been a crazy summer, really. He thought about the fence around the lighthouse, and the Galindo kids, and the ice cream truck. Then he thought about Chase Kark and his lies, and unbidden, his thoughts returned to what had happened at town hall. He tried to keep his thoughts on the good stuff, like the fact they'd have the lighthouse back, but Sheldon's sneer kept popping up. Jax scowled, wrapping his arms around his stomach.

Dad's arm tightened on his shoulders. "What are you thinking about?" he asked.

Jax didn't answer for a minute. Then he shrugged and said, "Just stupid Kark and his stupid friends." He didn't say anything more, but Dad held him close.

"They were some pretty nasty people," he said. "There was Kark, who doesn't care about the island or its history. And there was his associate—"

"Sheldon. His name was Sheldon," Jax interrupted. He wasn't sure he'd ever forget that guy's name.

Dad hugged him. "Sheldon. He was not only a crook and a liar but also a terrible, racist, bigoted one. I wish I could say he's the only one out there, but unfortunately there are plenty more." He sighed.

Jax didn't say anything. The stomachache feeling was coming back.

"Jackson." Dad turned so that he could look right into Jax's eyes.

Jax looked back at him. Dad was tanner than during the school year, his hair longer and messier than usual. But his blue-gray eyes and sandy-brown hair still looked nothing like Jax's. Jax tried to look away.

"Jackson," Dad repeated. "There are more good ones than bad. More Captain Jims and Officer Levees and Natalia Galindos and Elon Reynoldses than there are Sheldons. I wish there were none of him. Seriously, if I could have one wish that would probably be it."

"I would wish for an invisibility cloak," Eli interrupted.

He was sitting behind them, listening. “Think of how we could get back at Sheldon if we had that! Poison ivy leaves rubbed on the inside of his clothes. Burrs stuck in his hair.”

“I would paste him when he was walking on Main Street,” Sam interrupted, a gleam in his eye. He had taken out one earbud to listen to the conversation. “Seriously. Stupid racist jerk. I’d just wait till he was rushing somewhere in those idiotic boat shoes, then I’d throw out my foot and BOOM! All over the sidewalk.” He smiled at the thought and held out his fist for Jax to bump. “Seriously, dude, that guy is a waste of oxygen. You’re worth a dozen of him. Just ignore him.”

Jax started to smile. With Jax’s permission, Papa had given the older Fletcher boys a brief overview of what had happened at town hall, but Jax hadn’t really wanted to talk about it with them. Now, though, even if they couldn’t totally understand, their righteous anger on his behalf felt really good.

“Hey! Next year can Jax and I do a sleepover in the lighthouse, just us?” Eli asked. “Maybe for my birthday!”

“If you do a double sleepover, then I get to do one by myself,” Sam said. “After all, I’m the oldest.”

“What about me?” Frog said, worming his way onto Dad’s lap. “I want a sleepover too! But not by myself—too scary! Can we do one all together?”

Everyone started talking at once. Dad tried to interrupt; then Papa said, "I think Dad and I get the first sleepover in the lighthouse next year! You maniacs can take the house!"

The boys gave such a chorus of approval that Sir Puggleton started barking.

Jax laughed and leaned back against the bench.

In the distance, Rock Island was getting smaller and smaller, its beaches and the town impossible to see against the dazzling blue of sea and sky. But Jax could still see the lighthouse, standing tall and striped above the horizon.

He shoved his hands in his pockets and watched the island recede. Then his hand brushed something square and folded. In one pocket was Alex's phone number and email address, which she had given him. But the other . . . he pulled it out and found a piece of paper, folded and twisted so that it looked like a boat. On it Elon had written a note.

> Glad to have seen the famous Fletcher Rock Island, and especially glad to have been here with your whole crowd. It's a great place, but can we agree, brother to brother, that it's not the most welcoming to dudes who look like us? Tell you what, next time you come to New York, you let me know. We'll take a little field trip: hear some music or watch some ball or eat some good grub. And I promise you that

you'll fit right in. Meanwhile, a little memento of your summer.

Folded up in the note was Chase Kark's official Rock Island parking permit.

Jax burst out laughing. His family crowded around him, trying to look at what was cracking him up.

Jax just held up the permit. "Elon must have pinched it from Kark and put it in my pocket when he hugged me goodbye! Classic."

Papa and Dad were laughing too, though Papa was shaking his head. "Great. My sister finally finds a terrific guy and he has mild criminal tendencies. Typical. I suppose we should mail it back, but . . ."

"Nah. Let him sweat it out," Dad said. "Any headache that man has is well deserved."

The early-morning sun was fully up by now, and the boat moved quickly toward the mainland. Jax let his thoughts run to the school year ahead, when he and Eli would once again be together at Shipton Upper Elementary. Sam started talking about the Shipton Elite soccer schedule, and Eli began to lobby hard for Chinese food for dinner, and Frog wondered loudly whether Birdy the turtle, who had spent the summer with their neighbor Mr. Nelson, had been lonely while they were gone.

But one by one, they fell silent, watching the island as it shimmered in the distance. Soon it disappeared into the blaze of sunlight. The day was glorious. The salt smell in the air and the slap of water against the boat spoke of beach days and summertime, but their thoughts were on their lives waiting for them at home. It was always a little sad to leave, but exciting too, to get to the place that lay ahead. And the island, they knew, would be waiting for them when they returned.

ACKNOWLEDGMENTS

I acknowledge that having kids, parents, librarians, and the great wide world read my first book was a wild and wonderful experience, and I'm so grateful that some of you came back for more. Early cheerleaders for the family Fletcher, like Carol Chittenden, retired owner of Eight Cousins Bookstore in Falmouth, and Christopher Rose, teacher and book buyer for Hugo Books in Andover, made me feel that even if no one else ever read it, the journey was worth it.

I acknowledge that it takes a village to make a book, and that the team at Delacorte Press, led by the amazing Beverly Horowitz, has done an incredible job. Heather Lockwood Hughes took my words and whipped them into shape with the precision skills found only in copy editors. (And neurosurgeons. Maybe she moonlights.) Tamar Schwartz kept everything rolling along like a Rock Island ferry. Kate Gartner, art director extraordinaire, created the beauty that is this book, and found Rebecca Ashdown, whose vision of the Fletcher boys matches my own so perfectly. Jillian Vandall, who is never bossy but often the boss, got all sorts of smart folks reading my books. This team took a story and made it a book.

I acknowledge that Krista Vitola deserves to be feted with gluten-free whoopie pies and champagne for being, without fail, the most responsive, positive, and enthusiastic editor I could imagine. The Fletchers and I are lucky to have her.

I acknowledge that Marietta "Z-Fresh" Zacker is a true coconspirator, partner, mentor, and friend. While I am still waiting for her to take me to Culebra so we can reenact the Lift from *Dirty Dancing,* she is a woman of her word and I have every confidence it will happen. After all, she has made all my other dreams come true.

I acknowledge that the writers' community, both online and in real life, has sustained me and made me a better writer and a better human. In particular, the We Need Diverse Books campaign and its founders have encouraged me to read broadly and widely, and showed me that frustration with the status quo can lead to positive change.

I also acknowledge that I waste an inordinate amount of time carousing around the interwebs with this aforementioned writers' community. To the OneFourKidLit group, and my super-sekrit writing lair LBs, and those I know and love on the Twitter: thank you for amusing me, supporting me, galvanizing me to write, and putting up with my photos of tiny owls wearing hats.

I acknowledge that Mega-Friend Kate Boorman has to endure more of this amusing, supporting, galvanizing, and owls-with-hats-gazing than the rest of the Internet put together, and I am so very grateful. Boris, I thank you.

Finally, I acknowledge my family: marauders, cheerleaders, and comrades-in-arms. Summers are about toes in the sand and the sting of salt water in the eyes. My parents taught me how to dive under the big waves and ride the smaller ones, my sister picked me up when I misjudged and got thrashed by sand and spray, and today Patrick, Noah, and Isabel join me in the sea, porpoising and surfing and splashing with joyful abandon. Thank you.

ABOUT THE AUTHOR

Dana Alison Levy was raised by pirates but escaped at a young age and went on to earn a degree in aeronautics and puppetry. Actually, that's not true—she just likes to make things up. That's why she has always wanted to write books. She was born and raised in New England and studied English literature before going to graduate school for business. While there is value in all learning, if she had known she would end up writing for a living, she might not have struggled through all those statistics and finance classes.

Dana was last sighted romping with her family in Massachusetts. If you need to report her for excessive romping, or if you want to know more, check out danaalisonlevy.com.